EARLY DAYS AT EMMERDALE FARM

A Star Original

D1581375

In *Annie Sugden's Country Diary*, Annie told of her life as a child and young woman in Beckindale, up to the time of her marriage to Jacob Sugden.

Early Days at Emmerdale Farm takes up the story in 1947 — Annie is expecting her first child and looking forward to a great future in post-War Britain. Of course, nothing ever turns out quite as planned, and Annie finds that things must get worse before they get better.

This book forms a fascinating backdrop to the regular Emmerdale Farm novels and the TV series on which they are based — but *Early Days* is also a lively and heart-warming story in itself.

EARLY DAYS AT EMMERDALE FARM

Lee Mackenzie

Emmerdale Farm is the successful
Yorkshire Television series
originated by Kevin Laffan

A STAR BOOK

published by
the Paperback Division of
W. H. ALLEN & Co. Ltd.

A Star Book
Published in 1979
by the Paperback Division of
W.H. Allen & Co. Ltd
A Howard and Wyndham Company
44 Hill Street, London W1X 8LB

Copyright © Trident Television,
a member of the Trident Television Group, 1979
Copyright © Lee Mackenzie, 1979

Printed in Great Britain by
Hunt Barnard Printing Ltd., Aylesbury, Bucks.

ISBN 0 352 30434 0

CHAPTER ONE

WHEN I REALISED I was expecting my first baby, I was very happy, in the way all women are when they think about having a wanted child. Moreover, I felt it would be good for my husband Jacob to be a father; I hoped it would steady him down, for he was very restless in those days.

And not without cause. The winter that had just gone by was one of the very worst this country has ever had. These days you often see headlines in the papers: *Worst in Living Memory*. Well, all I can say is, folk must have short memories, for I haven't lived through a worse spell of weather than that winter.

In my diary, which I still kept up, though not as regularly as when I was a girl, I noted: 'Funny how difficult it is to get coal. Now the war's over you'd think supplies would be better.'

They weren't. They were worse, much worse. We'd got

used to funny coal during the war, called 'nutty slack' – I remember comedian Jack Train used to make puns about it on the radio. It was terrible stuff, burned very slow and low, but at least you got it. But now the war was over, and the coalman kept saying: 'Sorry, there's nothing in the coalyard.'

We weren't so badly off as some, I agree. We had an old kitchen range at Emmerdale, which would obligingly take twigs and billets of wood. But you know, you've got to go out fetching wood if you're going to use it as a fuel, and my husband had the farm to see to. To help him he had my father, in his so-called leisure hours; Dad, of course, was still working up at Verney's. And in the winter, your day is limited by the light. You can't go out foraging for wood after work if it's pitch dark. The other helper on the farm was our land-girl, Molly Pepwith; she was sent to us by the Ministry of Agriculture and Fisheries, a nice lass, hard-working but of course, not really born to farmwork. She would do anything she was told to, but she often had to be shown, so that was a bit of a tie to Jacob.

Everybody began to be worried about the fuel supplies. I remember the head of one of the Electricity Boards – I think it was Birmingham – stated out loud: 'We are heading towards a national calamity.' We all kept expecting something to be done. What, I don't know, because if there weren't enough miners to get the coal, there couldn't be an increase in supplies. That seemed to be the problem: not enough miners, not enough equipment – many of the miners hadn't gone back to the pits when they left the forces, and the equipment hadn't been renewed since 1938.

I think the first factory to close down for lack of coal was the Austin Motor Company. Mr Shinwell, the Minister of Fuel, started a rationing scheme; he called it 'allocation' but it was fuel rationing – to factories, I mean. Two weeks later he cut the allowance by half. 'I don't understand how a minister can make an allowance one week and cut it so hard a fortnight later,' I wrote in bewilderment in my diary.

Nobody else understood it either. Us country bumpkins,

who were accustomed to looking ahead, just watched with amazement while we seemed to lurch towards disaster. Yet the government seemed to think 'everything would turn out all right in the end'.

Perhaps it would have. But that was without taking the weather into account. It had been getting colder all over Christmas but then, on the 27th January, the temperature really dropped, far below zero. I believe I'm right in saying it was colder in Britain that winter than it was in Iceland.

Nobody in the countryside is surprised by cold weather. It's part of the cycle of the seasons. But even Beckindale was taken aback by the severity of that first day. The very milk froze in the churns. I've never known that happen before. You could hear frozen milk chinking about inside the churns when you moved them.

How did it come about that I heard frozen milk knocking against the side of the containers? Because I was moving them to help Jacob. The collection lorry didn't arrive. He was very anxious that day and the next, because a small milk-producer only has a limited number of churns, and if the lorry didn't come to collect the full ones and bring empties, he was going to be in a fix.

The radio said ice on the roads was making conditions very bad. On the night of the 28th, it snowed. Then the snow froze. Traffic everywhere began to come to a standstill. People couldn't get to work. Miners couldn't get to the pits, which only made matters worse. The electricity supply began to be cut.

Now, Jacob had spent his precious gratuity – the sum paid out to him when he left the Navy – on having electricity brought to Emmerdale. Only to the milking parlour, you understand; he couldn't afford to have the farmhouse wired up, and I quite accepted that. But he had hoped that electricity in the mistle would make it possible for him to increase his herd. Now the power kept going off, without warning. He had to milk by hand. And he had to teach poor Molly to do it, too. She did her best, poor girl, but the beasts didn't like her. I think they sensed she was nervous.

So of course I took over her chores in the mistle while she went into my kitchen to do the cooking – and she was a terrible cook.

When I look back on it now, I suppose it has its comic side. I'd be stripping Blossom Three, and I'd smell this terrible aroma of burnt potatoes and go dashing into the house, to find that Molly had snatched the pot off the range and burnt her hand on the handle. So I'd have to put salve on her fingers, and pick up the pot, and scrape burnt potatoes off the floor – oh, my clean floor! — and rush back to finish Blossom Three, and then come in to get something ready for the men's tea.

On the 30th January, we had a blizzard. I can truly say I've never seen anything like it, before or since. The wind tore across the dale at what was afterwards reported as sixty miles an hour. The snow was blowing absolutely horizontally, for hours on end.

Villages all over the country were cut off by snow-drifts. Beckindale was cut off from Hotten, Hotten was cut off from Leeds and Bradford. We, of course, were cut off from everywhere. Emmerdale Farm stuck up out of the top of a snow-drift that rose around it like a great, enfolding wad of cotton wool. We couldn't get out through the front door – but of course, we almost always use the kitchen door anyway, and though that had a snow-drift outside, it was fairly easy to dig away.

My father set out as usual for Verney's, but came back about two hours later, blue with cold and exhausted. He'd only done about half a mile, and what was worse, he'd lost his sense of direction. 'I didn't know whether I was heading north or south,' he told me in a quaking voice. 'I never was so frightened in my life, Annie. I thought I was going to die out there in the cold.'

Luckily, as he threshed about in the drifts he'd seen the outline of Grey Top, the big crag about half a mile to the west of Emmerdale, and using that to get his bearings he'd come home. He was soaked and weary, but would have started out again for Verney's if I hadn't hung on to his arm and begged him not to. 'But the stock, Annie! Someone's got to feed the stock!'

'There are other folk at Verney's, Dad. Bide here until it's safe to get about.'

I don't know when I expected that would be. I suppose I thought that, as usual, we'd have a thaw in a day or two. But nothing of the kind. Icicles developed on the edge of the roof, hung from trees, prevented the gate from opening. Electricity went off completely. Our radio ran on a big dry battery, so we were still able to get the news, which was universally bad. Trams in the towns had stopped (we still had trams in those days). Electric trains weren't running. Even steam trains weren't moving much; one news bulletin reported that the Cornish Riviera Express (express!) had taken eight and a half hours to get to London and when the frozen passengers staggered off, looking for a hot cup of tea at the refreshment room, they found a cardboard notice on the door: 'No Tea, No Coffee, No *gas!*'

We had another blizzard on 5th February. I noted in my diary: 'It's strange to see that the new fall of snow shows up as a different colour from what has been lying – because the old snow has frozen so hard it has a bluish tint.' I'd also looked up and copied a verse by Shakespeare:

When icicles hang by the wall
And Dick, the shepherd, blows his nail,
And Tom bears logs into the hall
And milk comes frozen home in pail,
When blood is nipped and ways be foul,
Then nightly sings the staring owl
Tu-whoo.

Things hadn't changed much in the three hundred years, it seemed to me! We'd got all those things happening except that I didn't hear the owl hoot. We don't have owls at Emmerdale, though there are some down towards Beckindale.

As to Dick the shepherd blowing his nails – Jacob was by way of being our shepherd, and he was worried about our sheep. He wasn't so interested in them as in the milk herd, but he'd inherited a flock from his father so naturally he wanted to make something of it. They were a hardy hill breed, and they don't come down to the valley unless the weather is going to be really terrible – and we ought to have taken warning because they'd been drifting down since Twelfth Night. They found enough to browse on in the valleys but once the snow came, they were soon going to starve. The snow covered everything, and far too deeply for even hungry sheep to push through.

So Jacob and my father began trudging out looking for them, and digging them out, and taking fodder to them. I don't think anyone who hasn't done it can understand how exhausting it is. You don't just walk out along a road, find a sheep standing there, and give it a handful of hay. You have to wade into the drifts, prodding with a stick to see if there's anything buried there, and then you have to find a way of getting them out. Even once you've dug an opening, the sheep may be so exhausted that you have to lift her out – and if you've ever tried lifting a sheep whose fleece is weighted with moisture you know what I mean when I say it takes muscle power.

Moreover, the sheep were supposed to find their own feedstuffs. They were supposed to eat the tough mountain grass. To keep them alive, my husband had to give them food that ought to have gone to the cattle. For every mouthful they ate, one less would go to the dairy herd – and they were supposed to help by pasturing in some sheltered land we kept for them as a winter meadow. That was six feet under the snow. So the dairy cows were eating hay and bought foodstuffs, intended as a supplement to their diet and not a mainstay.

As if that wasn't worry enough, there was the milk itself. We ran out of churns on 1st February and from then on I was scouring and scalding every container I could lay hands on. Pails, tin baths, mixing bowls, preserving pans, china plant pots from the front parlour, jugs and jam jars, even flower vases.

'We'll be at the stage of using teacups soon,' Jacob

sighed, as I teetered out to him over the frozen yard with my arms full of ewers and basins from the bedrooms.

You have to understand that we had no plastic in those days. Like most people, I shake my head at the litter of plastic bags I see lying around in city streets and even on farmland – but plastic is a blessing. If worst comes to worst these days, we can always put the milk in some big container like a trough, by lining it with suitable plastic first. But in the days immediately after the war, the 'plastics revolution' hadn't really happened. I'd only just heard of nylon, for instance – never seen it, only heard of it. I think I'd seen a plastic raincoat. But we just didn't have any kind of material that would have helped us store that milk.

In a way it was easy to store. It froze solid, so there was no chance of its going sour. But the day would come when we'd have to pour it away. That, to a farmer, is almost unthinkable. But luckily the yield was going down anyway, because of the shortage of feed.

I say luckily . . . There wasn't anything lucky about it. Less milk means less income.

Jacob grew gaunt and pale with worry. His gypsy good looks were accentuated by it, but that was no consolation to him or to me.

We'd sit in the kitchen by the light of the fire – because we ran out of paraffin and couldn't get any more – and murmur about what we ought to do. But, really, there wasn't anything we could do at present. We just had to wait until the weather relented. From what we heard on our radio, everybody else was having just as bad a time. All the street lamps were out in the towns, escalators didn't go up or down, lifts weren't working, supplies of candles had run out. I heard afterwards that Mr Rosewell, our vicar, opened his cupboard and took out his store of church candles, which he carried round the village, giving one to each household until he ran out.

Food prices soared in the cities. Supplies of vegetables couldn't be got to the shops, even if they could have been dug out of the ground or the clamps. Food was still rationed, you know. In fact, there was less on the ration than there had been during the war.

That's a thing I'd like to mention. Youngsters who ask about the war seem to imagine that on VE Day, everything went back to normal. True, the lights went on at night; there was no more blackout. But rationing went on. And on, and on. What was worse, it got more severe. We got less meat, butter cooking fat, and cheese than we had had while the war was going on.

The reason is obvious. Shipping losses during the war had been enormous. There simply weren't the cargo ships to bring food supplies, and now that men were going back to their own countries those countries wanted their food supplies for themselves. So if Britain wanted food, Britain would have to pay higher prices. But Britain hadn't any money.

We were in a 'crisis' about the economy. It seems to me we've been in a 'crisis' almost ever since.

During that terrible winter, food was really scarce. I don't mean that people actually starved – although in villages that were cut off I think household supplies were used up before the lorries got through. Even the scanty food ration wasn't available, supposing you could get to the shop where you were 'registered' to present your ration book.

Just for the record, food rationing didn't end until 1954. Nine years after the end of the war! These days, when things get bad and folk go round saying, 'Isn't it awful? How are we ever going to make ends meet?' I go to the old chocolate box in which I keep a few mementoes, and I take out my wartime ration book. Some people made a bonfire of them when rationing ended, and I understand the impulse that made them do it. But I kept mine, and I look at it, and remember that winter, and I know that these days we're well-off compared with the immediate post-war years.

Of course even on an isolated farm, it's difficult to starve. I've always kept hens and geese, so we had eggs and poultry. Besides, if you live in a place where the roads can become impassable, you have enough sense to keep some stores. I had enough flour to last a month, and yeast, which can be made at home if you have to, and salt, and though I didn't have sugar or dried fruit I had honey and home-made preserves. I could always make bread and cakes, even on the worst days. The kitchen range was a bit temperamental on its diet of twigs and logs, but I managed. We ran out of tea, which was rationed, so I couldn't have a big store of it; but we drank milk – we had plenty of that!

The day the bulldozer got through to us, we ran down to the lane-end and cheered. Pete Swanlett, who was driving, stood up in his cab and bowed. We took him indoors and plied him with home-made rhubarb wine, so that when he backed out of the lane, he was a bit mazed in the head and fetched up through the stone wall into the paddock. But we didn't mind.

I got a lift on the bulldozer down to the village so as to stock up on goods I'd run short of – things like mustard, and our ration of tea and sugar.

For the next few days we plodded about in the slush, trying to get back to something like normal. Jacob's milk stores were taken away – some of it would be lost, no doubt, but much of it would be all right once it had been pasteurised. We spent a hectic day pouring the milk from our funny containers into churns, so that it could go to the processing plant.

I walked into Beckindale each day, to catch up on the news and re-stock my larder. I got Jacob to bring paraffin home in the farm truck, because I didn't want to be trapped without any light in the evenings – I can knit in the dark, but for sewing and mending I needed a decent light.

I took the bus into Hotten to get a new battery for the radio. Ours was just beginning to run down when the thaw released us from captivity – and it wouldn't have been pleasant to be completely without news.

If this all sounds as if I was getting ready for the next disaster, you're right. You see, us farming folk knew something that the town-dwellers had forgotten. Snow is after all water, and water has to go somewhere. Where it goes is into the soil. It seeps through to the fissures in the rocks and runs into rivers. *But* – the river is only a certain depth between its banks. It can cope with an influx of new water to a certain level, but after that the river will overflow.

Subconsciously the country people were aware of all this. We knew that the thaw wasn't the end of our troubles. It was like a lull in the battle: the final stage of the war of the winter was still to come.

Torrential rain began to pour down on us. It wasn't cold enough for snow now, so we got rain instead. Added to the melted snow, the amount of water going to the rivers was tremendous.

The rain ruined our remaining haystacks at Emmerdale. In those days we made hay in the old way, and stacked it outdoors in beautifully built stacks like yellow houses without doors or windows. The melting snow and ice seeped into them, the rain poured down on them, and they disintegrated. The cords couldn't hold the stooks together any more; they rotted or gave way under the weight of the sodden hay.

My father got back from Verney's to find Jacob standing by the light of a lantern, staring at the wreckage of the stackyard. He put a hand on his sagging shoulder.

'Don't thee fret too much, lad,' he said, intending to comfort him. 'Mr Verney's saying he'll see his neighbours all reet for feed if they need it.'

Jacob turned on him, almost snarling. 'I dunna want to be beholden to Verney or any ither man! All I want is to run my own farm, if the Almighty will relent long enough to let me do it.'

'Jacob!' My father was shocked at what he felt was blasphemy.

'Come away, Dad,' I murmured. 'It isn't the time to talk to him about the future.'

'The future!' Jacob cried. 'Have we got a future here? You tell me! One-third of the sheep dead, the milk yield reduced, the herd in poor condition after the cold weather and the shortage of food, and now the hay's gone . . .'

There seemed nothing to say. I did my best to make things better by preparing a good meal that evening. Molly, our Land Girl, came trudging up from the beck to say that the water seemed to be coming down very fast by the old wool bridge – the bridge the woolpackers used to take with their pack horses.

'Did you go by the old mill?' I asked. 'There's a measure on the wall there.'

'No, I'll go first thing in the morning to check,' Molly said.

But she didn't, because next day the water was up to the spot where the road dips close to the old bridge. She came running back up the lane, the rain beating down on her wide-brimmed hat.

'Mr Sugden, Mr Sugden, come quickly!'

Jacob, sweeping rain water out of the mistle, threw down his broom and ran to join her. They disappeared from my view; I was washing up in the kitchen, but watched through the window until they came back.

Jacob was yards ahead of Molly. He came rushing in. 'Annie! The water's up over the wool bridge.'

'Over it? How do you mean?'

'The wood bridge is covered. You can scarcely see it.'

The wood bridge had a very low parapet but even so, it stood about four feet above the surface of the beck. That meant that the water had risen four feet overnight.

All that day the water level kept moving relentlessly up. I went down to Beckindale to fetch the last of my replacement supplies. I didn't need to buy bread, but I had to have flour and oatmeal; I used up the last of my available 'BUs' on those, because I had a feeling it would be a long time before I could get more. 'BUs' were Bread Units, coupons that were clipped out when you bought anything made with flour, or flour itself.

Were the floods worse than the blizzards? Perhaps not. At least you could get about in the floods, if you had a boat. There were about half a dozen rowboats in Beckindale, mostly used by the anglers. The police commandeered those and ferried people about, but it was precarious and uncomfortable. I made two trips by rowboat, one to see Mr Rosewell and one to fetch veterinary supplies for Jacob. It seemed silly to me to be going out and about, using up space in a boat which might be needed for someone else.

But for the animals the floods were tragic. They drowned in the surging waters, or were isolated to starve to death on knolls and hillsides. Jacob made a raft from old fencing and fetched in some of the sheep, but he had a hard time getting them on to the gimcrack affair and lost two or three who simply wouldn't keep still – they fell off into the water and he couldn't get them back.

He grew more and more grim as the floods went on. My diary is full of figures, noting the water level. 'River Wissey in Norfolk has overflowed its banks and flooded the Fens – eight thousand acres seem to be under water at one go.' 'Eleven feet of water in Hotten – Constable Brownley says Hotten Parish Church is flooded up to the altar table.' 'Emmerdale Beck is up ten and a half feet, water has reached the four-acre field.'

At last, on the 4th April, I see I've noted: 'Trent, Ouse, Don, Derwent and Humber have burst their banks. The City of York is under seventeen feet of water. Water at Emmerdale is going down rapidly.'

The reason for the last remark is, of course, that Emmerdale and Beckindale were higher than the Vale of York. The Dales began to dry out before the plains. What was good news for us was bad news for low-lying areas.

But you should have seen what was left! It looked like one great sea of mud. Mud and marshes – that was Beckindale valley after the floods receded. The financial loss to Yorkshire farms was reputed to be in the neighbourhood of a million pounds.

It was into that ruined landscape that Laurence Stanton came, hoping to find the girl he'd loved during the war and to take her back with him to South America. I sent him away; what else could I do? I was a married woman, expecting her husband's baby.

I don't deny I was unsettled and unhappy for a few weeks after that meeting with Laurence. But there was so much to do at Emmerdale! The depredations of the bad weather had to be made good.

Jacob had lost a little over half his sheep. He had managed to keep all the milk herd safe, but he had had to pour away milk – this time it really was impossible to save it, for we couldn't scour and scald the containers because our water supply was damaged by the flood. There would be compensation to some extent, but it wouldn't come at once and wouldn't be equal to the losses he'd suffered.

My father did his best to help, but he daren't say too much. Working as he did at a big farm like Verney's, he could have reported a more hopeful picture – but that would only have made my husband more resentful. Dad helped Jacob rebuild the flood-ruined walls and mend the leaks in the roofs where the torrential rain had slipped the slates. He helped remake drainage channels. He helped bury the drowned sheep.

For my part, I put the mud-soaked clothes into the wash-copper and got them clean; I dried them and pressed them and mended them. I looked after my geese and poultry with extra care, so that when Easter came I was able to sell dyed Easter eggs to Potterton's of Hotten and had a little sum of money to contribute. Profits from the poultry are traditionally considered to be the pocket money of the farmer's wife, but in these circumstances I didn't dream of keeping it for Easter finery. I put it in the kitty.

Really, everything looked a bit gloomy. Then, one morning, I switched on my radio as usual to listen while I did the washing up. The men had gone out to their work, Molly was upstairs in her room sorting out some underwear for dabbing-out. The announcer said something about a new musical show that had come on in London the previous evening, and then said he'd play a tune from the show.

And out of my radio came this wonderful man's voice, rich and clear, singing:

'*Oh, what a beautiful morning,*

2

Oh, what a beautiful day!
I've got a wonderful feeling
Everything's going my way!'

In general I'm not one for 'moods'. I suppose I'm what's called 'equable'. But I'd been depressed for the last few weeks — perhaps because of the dreadful weather, perhaps simply because the hormone balance had altered because of the baby that was coming. Whatever the reason, I must admit I'd felt life was a bit weary at that time.

But then I heard this song. I looked up from my washing up, and out of the window I saw the pear tree blossom beginning to tip the branches with a pearly sheen. The sun was shining. A blackbird was singing from the boughs of the beech tree.

All at once light seemed to shine in on me. What had I to be unhappy about? I had a home, a husband who loved me, a father still spared to me, I'd survived a war that had killed millions of others, and I was expecting a baby.

It was downright wicked to be depressed. There was an old hymn we used to sing at Sunday School: 'Count your blessings, name them one by one . . .' During the three minutes that the record of the song lasted, I named my blessing one by one — and I was shamed before my Maker.

I never saw the stage show from which that song came, so I never saw him, that singer with the beautiful, manly voice. His name was Howard Keel, I believe. I don't suppose he knows what a difference he made to me that day with his song. You see? We just don't know what effect our actions will have, do we? That song, and the strong, clear tones in which it was sung, were just the pick-me-up I needed.

The National Health Service hadn't really got going in those days, and even if it had, there were so many babies being born that the hospitals couldn't cope. Nowadays it's taken for granted that an expectant mother will have her baby in hospital, and in fact if she doesn't want to, she has to put up quite a fight to have it at home. What a strange reversal it seems from my young days! I wasn't even asked if I wanted to have my baby at home. It was taken as read.

Only if I had been ill would I have gone into the maternity ward.

I'll admit that my doctor, Dr Anstruther, was a bit put out when he called on me at Emmerdale and found we didn't have either electricity or gas for hot water. 'Good God, woman, are you living in the Dark Ages?' he exclaimed in exasperation. 'What's your husband thinking about? Why doesn't he have electricity put into the house?'

'He will, when we can afford it,' I replied. 'But in the meantime, if it's hot water you want, the kitchen range never goes out – we have constant hot water.' I smiled a little as I said it, and Dr Anstruther relented.

'Well, all right, all right. I suppose farmers' wives have been bringing babies into the world in isolated places like this for long enough . . . So long as you're fit and well, everything will be all right, I'm sure.'

The District Midwife, Miss Spenlow, wasn't the least bit worried by our lack of amenities. She was used to it. When I murmured that Dr Anstruther wasn't pleased, she shrugged.

'Just like a man,' she said. 'Clinical and taken up with the trimmings. What's important is that the mother is healthy and happy. I've always found that women like to be in their own homes when they're having their babies. Hospitals can be intimidating places.' She nodded at me, so that her pork-pie hat tilted forward on her round forehead. 'We'll manage fine, you and me, Mrs Sugden.'

And so we did. I had to send Molly Pepwith pedalling away like mad to fetch the midwife when the time came, but she came cycling back with Miss Spenlow alongside. Funny, to look back. Midwives and District Nurses all travelled by bike. I don't think it ever occurred to them that they ought to have cars. I must say I had a grin to myself when I saw the two of them, pedalling into the yard, Miss Spenlow like a neat little waterhen in her dark blue gaberdine, and Molly like an untidy thrush in her tawny breeches and pullover.

Jacob was pleased and proud when he got home from the

upper field to find he was the father of a seven-and-a-half pound son. He was waiting when my father got back, a glass of brandy in his hand.

I could hear him in the kitchen: 'A toast, Father-in-law, to your grandson!'

'A boy?' Dad cried. 'Is he all right? Is Annie –?'

'Mother and child both doing well,' Jacob cried. 'Come on, drink up!'

'I'll just pop up and see her first –'

'No, no, she's supposed to be having a sleep. Drink up.'

Having a sleep! As if I could sleep with that noise going on downstairs. But I lay back, smiling at the delight in his voice.

It seemed to make all the difference to Jacob. He picked up hope and energy from the birth of his son. Moreover, things seemed to improve. The government brought in a bill guaranteeing settled prices for farm produce, which seemed to make the prospects better. There was even a clause promising special help to farmers on marginal and hill land. Then there had been some actual money in compensation for the lost sheep and the flood damage. And the milk herd had picked up. And the hay harvest had been good. And the barley, which he was just getting in, was in good heart.

All in all, Jacob felt life was improving. As if to crown it, he now had a son.

It was a good thing he couldn't foresee at that moment the anxiety we were to undergo before the year was out. At that moment, he had no foreboding of the illness that was to threaten our baby.

CHAPTER TWO

HAPPEN I'VE GIVEN the impression that the only good thing that happened that year was the birth of our little boy. That's not quite true, although it was a hard time for everybody. Because of that very fact, the government sponsored an exhibition called 'Britain Can Make It', which I suppose had two aims – to cheer us all up and to show the rest of the world that though we were staggering around a bit after the war, we were still capable of delivering the goods.

It came on at the Victoria and Albert Museum in London in the autumn, opened by the King and Queen. But there were mini-exhibitions in various provincial centres, and one of those was Bradford. Bradford was celebrating the centenary of its city charter – I think the full name for it was the Charter of Incorporation. Funny to think that Bradford had only been around for a hundred years! Of course there had always been a community in that area; someone told me during the centenary celebrations that there had been a church of some kind on the site of Bradford Cathedral since the seventh century. But what I mean is that in one specific year Queen Victoria granted a charter to the town council, making it a city and enabling the mayor to be styled Lord Mayor. So Bradford was having a bit of a celebration.

There were concerts and shows and processions, beginning at the start of July. The Britain Can Make It Exhibition became a part of the celebration too.

Then another nice thing that came about that year was the New Look. I'll take a wager that a lot more people have heard of the New Look than the Britain Can Make It Exhibition! Somehow it seems to have stuck in the mind. Perhaps it's because newspapers adopted it as a phrase – if politicians tried some new approach, if car designers brought out a new model, it was always a New Look.

The original 'New Look' was the name given to a set of fashion designs by a man called Christian Dior. I read about him in the papers and looked at the rather muzzy photographs, and all I could say was that the clothes he had designed would take up all my clothing coupons for about the next five years! The journalists told me that the skirt of one of his dresses had nearly sixty yards of material in it. Daft, it seemed to me.

But you know – it's funny – although it all seemed so impractical, it had an effect on women. We had been so accustomed to the rather straight lines of the clothes we'd been wearing that we shied away from the gathers and curves of the New Look. But once we 'got our eye in' we began to see you didn't actually need sixty yards of cloth. All you had to do was make everything a bit less square.

Comedian Bob Hope said something that was very true, as well as being funny. Interviewed on, I think, 'In Town Tonight' on radio, he was asked what he thought about the New Look. He replied: 'I'm still giving the old look to women!' And in a way he put his finger on it – all that was happening was that women were going back to what they used to look like. During the war we'd been wearing what was almost a uniform – straight skirt coming just below the knees, close fitting blouse or jacket, squarish shoulder line, everything very plain and untrimmed. Now we began to soften the line. If we were planning a new dress or a spring coat for next year, we began to think of something a bit less like the clothes the women's forces were wearing.

The reason I'm telling you all this is because these things persuaded Jacob to take me to Bradford for the day. He wanted to give me a bit of a celebration after Jack was born, and what with the high jinks going on for the centenary in the city, and the chance to see the shops with the famous New Look on display, he felt a trip to Bradford would be ideal.

The original plan was to leave baby Jack at home just for that day, in the care of our Molly Pepwith. She wasn't really keen, because she knew nothing about babies, and to tell the truth I wasn't really keen either because I was reluctant to leave my six-weeks-old treasure in her care. So after she ran a piece of wire into her hand and had to have it bandaged up, I wasn't really put out when Jacob said we'd have to take the baby with us.

Jack was as good as gold on the journey by bus and train to Bradford. Eh, dear me – when I think of it now – we used to have trains that went from Hotten to Bradford! But Dr Beeching cut them off when he was trying to 'improve' the railways.

Well, anyhow, we got to Bradford and we strolled around in the fine October weather. I can't deny I enjoyed it. We had our midday meal in a British Restaurant, which was one of those good ideas that eventually were done away with – cheap, nourishing food at a subsidised price. We went to the exhibition. We wandered in and out of the shops. I had some clothing coupons to spare; there was an extra allowance for maternity clothes and I hadn't used mine up, having been trained by my mother to adapt existing clothes by all sorts of tricks and stratagems.

So I bought three yards of Yorkshire tweed to make a coat for the winter, and was very pleased with myself. Jacob told me expense was no object but even so, I was careful to find something that was excellent value – eight shillings and elevenpence a yard! That's less than fifty pence in new money. Try buying Yorkshire tweed for that price today . . .

Our original intention had been to go to a show in the evening, but now we had the baby with us so we had to get home for his evening feed and bath. I was quite glad, really. I'd had enough for one day. Though I like Bradford, I found it tiring on that warm autumn day.

Next day I caught up with all the little household chores that seem to accumulate if you're away for a day. I showed my new tweed length to Molly, who was rightly envious. In the evening I played about with laying out the coat pattern on the material, to see how to cut it. Everything was really tranquil and comforting; I felt I was the luckiest woman in the world.

It was next morning that anxiety began to filter in among this rose-tinted haze. The baby wasn't well. He couldn't seem to keep his feed down. At first I didn't get too alarmed, because it seemed likely that the change to his routine had upset him. But when he didn't succeed in re-taining any food all day, I began to get worried.

During that night he cried a lot. I got up to him several times. The fourth time, I sat with him. I'd realised that he was very hot.

I didn't have a thermometer so I couldn't take his temperature, but I didn't need that to tell me he was running a fever. I sat by his crib thinking that if the temperature didn't drop by breakfast time, I'd better call the doctor.

I'm one of those who hate to trouble the doctor, unless it's something really serious. If I'd seen the slightest change for the better in Jack's sickness, I'd have waited. But while I was cooking the eggs and bacon for my father and my husband, I could hear Jack crying. And it came to me he was crying because he was in pain. It wasn't just that he felt sick; something was hurting him.

I asked Dad to ring the doctor from the phone box in the

village on his way to Verney's. We didn't have the phone then – it seems incredible to me that we managed without one until about five years ago.

'Tell Doctor that I think it's something serious, Dad,' I said to him as I wrapped his muffler around his neck before he stepped out into the morning mist.

He paused, looking at me in surprise. 'Serious, Annie?'

'I think so.'

We looked at each other. He put a hand momentarily on my shoulder. 'I'll come back then, and tell you when Doctor's coming.'

'Nay, don't do that. It's a long walk –'

'That's all right, Annie, I don't mind.'

Dr Anstruther sent word by my father that he'd be with me as soon as he'd seen his morning surgery. He had a young partner, Dr Boles, recently demobbed from the RAMC and very keen to catch up with civilian medicine, who actually turned up less than an hour later.

'Dr Anstruther was a bit worried,' he explained. 'He knew you wouldn't have rung him unless you felt it was important'.

'It's just that the baby seems to have been getting more and more feverish since yesterday morning.'

'Let's have a look, then,' he said, and followed me up to my bedroom.

Jack was lying in his crib making a little whining, exhausted cry. The skin of his face and brow were pink with high temperature. He was moving his head a little from side to side.

Dr Boles took his temperature and then asked me to pick him up and hold him on my lap. He examined him very carefully. I noticed how he extended his little legs and watched what happened as he let them go. He felt all over that tiny body with square, kindly hands.

After what seemed to me a century he told me to wrap Jack up in his shawl. 'I think he ought to go to hospital,' he said.

I was so shattered I couldn't speak. I thought he'd say,

'It's colic,' or 'It's a chill.' Hospital . . . what could be so serious that he had to go to hospital?

'We'll have to do some tests,' he went on. 'I'll get the cottage hospital to send an ambulance —'

'Oh, no, my husband can take me in the farm truck —'

'No, Mrs Sugden. The baby ought to go in an ambulance. It's important to have conditions as sterile as possible.'

'Why? What's wrong?'

'I'm not sure. I just want to see what the tests will show. I have to go now, but you get the baby ready for the ambulance. I'll meet you at the cottage hospital in about an hour and a half.'

It's funny how I'd felt I had to make tremendous preparations for the day in Bradford — cooking food in advance, making a list for Molly so she knew what to do. Now all at once all that seemed quite unimportant. I bathed the baby and tried to give him a feed, but he wouldn't take it. I held him carefully, because I could tell that it hurt him when I pressed him against me.

The ambulance came, we were whisked to the little hospital outside Hotten. There Jack was taken from me and put in a room by himsef. Dr Boles arrived sooner than he'd said, and began to question me. When he heard I'd spent a day in Bradfort two days previously, he frowned.

'Do you think he's caught some germ there?' I ventured.

'It could well be . . .'

Then, to my amazement, he began asking me how I felt. He said he'd like to examine me, and though I was a bit vexed and told him I was all right except worried about Jack, I went along with it.

'Well, you're all right,' he said. 'But I'd like you to stay here at the hospital for the rest of the day —'

'But why? What's the matter?'

'Nothing — with you. But your baby may be quite ill, and you may be incubating the same thing, Mrs Sugden. Is your husband quite fit?'

'Fit as a fiddle.' I was trying to be very brusque and sensible, but I could feel my throat tightening up. 'What is it you suspect, Dr Boles?'

'Let's not put names to things yet, Mrs Sugden. No sense in scaring you unnecessarily. It may all be a false alarm.'

But I was scared. I think now he'd have been better to tell me what he suspected. I saw that he had something serious in mind, and I noticed I was treated by the staff of the cottage hospital as if I were highly infectious. I was put in a room off the same corridor as the one in which Jack's room was. When I looked out of the door now and again, I saw that the nurses who went in there were wearing surgical masks.

There's something very frightening about a surgical mask. It seems to mean the patient is very ill. I sat there, cold with fright, not knowing what to do. I didn't want to be a nuisance to anybody by demanding an explanation of what was going on, but as the hours went by I got to the stage where I couldn't bear it.

I stood in the doorway of my room, and caught a blue-clad young woman who was hurrying past. She had a specially pleated cap on her head – I knew she was a sister. 'Please tell me what's happening,' I begged.

'Now, now,' she said. 'Come back in and sit down. You'll do no good by getting in a state –'

'I'm not in a state,' I said, although I was. 'I've been here for over three hours and nobody tells me anything – I want to know what's happening to my baby!'

'We're taking specimens –'

'Of what?' I cried. I don't know what I thought it meant.

'Well . . .' She hesitated. She could see I was determined to get some facts. 'We've withdrawn some cerebro-spinal fluid and it's gone to Bradford to be analysed –'

'I don't know what that means. Cerebro-spinal?'

'From the spinal cord.'

'What . . . what does that mean? Something is wrong with the baby's back? Is that it? I could tell he was in pain.'

'We'll know better when we get the results,' she said.

'When will that be?'

'This evening, I think.'

I found my brain was beginning to function again. 'I must get in touch with my husband,' I said. 'He's got no idea what is happening.'

'There's a telephone in the corridor, at the far end –'

'But we're not on the phone.'

'Oh.' She thought about that. 'I think the best thing would be for you to go home,' she murmured. 'We shan't get any news from Bradford until six or seven oclock. Don't you think it would be better to go home and explain everything to your husband and then both come back this evening?'

'Yes. Thank you.' I hesitated. 'Can I go in and see Jackie before I go?'

'No!' She shook her head with vehemence. 'No, better not.'

She let me peep at him from the doorway, but all I could see was a little hump in the cot, covered with a white flannelette blanket. He was still crying – the same tired, exhausted sound.

I walked into Hotten and took the bus home. It was mid-afternoon. Jacob was up on the east field, ploughing with the tractor lent to the farmers of Beckindale by the Ministry of Agriculture and Fisheries.

He switched off and came hurrying to me when he saw me. 'Well?'

'They don't know yet, Jacob.'

'Don't know? How d'you mean? Surely at a hospital –'

'But it's only a little place, Jacob. They're waiting for some special results from Bradford'. I explained it to him as best I could, and he put an arm round me. I could feel how tense he was, with anxiety.

'He's not really so very ill, is he, Annie?'

'I . . . I think he is.'

'But he's such a grand little lad.'

'Aye. Never a bit of trouble until yesterday . . .'

I kept busy until teatime. Molly undertook to do the washing up so I could get off to the hospital with Jacob. My father said, 'He'll be all right, Annie love. Don't fret.'

When we reached the cottage hospital the same sister was in the polished hall. I think she was waiting for us.

'Mrs Sugden.' She came quickly towards us, and spoke quietly. 'You're here very prompt.'

'This is my husband.'

'How do you do, Mr Sugden. Well, I'm afraid the news isn't very good. Baby has been taken to the special isolation unit at Connelton.'

'Isolation . . .?'

'We got the results an hour ago.' She laid a hand on my arm. 'It's infantile paralysis.'

Infantile paralysis . . . Even the name is different now. We call it polio, and thanks to the marvellous work of Dr Salk in America, we hardly fear it any more.

But in those days it was a name that struck terror into the hearts of parents.

For some unknown reason, that particular year had seen an absolute epidemic of the disease in Britain. I hadn't been paying particular attention because it all seemed to be happening in the big cities like London and Glasgow, but of course I'd seen reports in the newspapers and heard discussions on the radio. The outburst had began much earlier than usual – I think hot weather was the time when it usually struck, but it began in May that year.

We then had a very fine summer, which apparently helped the spread of the infection. It was caused not by a germ but a virus, if I remembered rightly. If I'd been taking notice, I'd have realised that during September there had been a big increase in the number of cases. Later, when of course I was keenly interested, I learned there had been nearly eight thousand cases. That was far, far more than we'd ever had before.

Now we know more about the disease, and children can be immunised against it. But at that time, it was a terrifying mystery. No one knew how it came about or how it spread. The symptoms were so like other illnesses that some cases were very serious indeed before they were recognised.

The death rate wasn't so bad as the fear of disability.

Muscles were paralysed, sometimes so completely that the patient couldn't breathe for himself and had to be helped by a machine. That was the year of the Iron Lung.

When Jacob and I got to the isolation unit at Connelton, they allowed us to look at Jack through a plate glass window. He was in a ward with three other tiny babies. A nurse, robed and masked, moved silently about among them.

I'd have given everything I had in the world to be allowed to go in and just touch him. But it wasn't permitted. We might take additional infection in with us, or catch the disease ourselves.

We stood there looking at the little cots. Jacob held my hand. We didn't speak.

That night I lay in bed praying, 'Don't let him be crippled.' The following night, after I'd been back to the hospital and seen the iron lung machine in a ward I passed, I prayed, 'Don't let him go into that, God. Please keep him from that.'

But when another two days had gone by I was praying, 'Let him live. Even if he can't walk – even if he can't move – let him live, dear Lord.'

Jacob couldn't forgive himself for having exposed Jack to the disease by taking him to Bradford. Any city was a likely source of infection; it was quite true that we ought not to have gone there with the baby, if we'd had any sense. But I kept begging him not to blame himself.

'Nobody could have foreseen this, Jacob. It's not your fault.'

'There was no need to go that day! We could have waited till Molly's hand was better and left him at home.'

'Who knows if he caught the sickness in Bradford, Jacob? There are cases in Hotten –'

'You know as well as I do that he took ill because we went on that day trip —'

'Nay, lad, don't take the blame on yourself. I wanted to go too.'

So it went on, talking it over and over. For three weeks

we went back and forth to the isolation unit, frightened each time that they'd tell us our baby had had to be put into the great tunnel-like machine to help him breathe.

Then, one Sunday afternoon, the little nurse who usually greeted us came to us with a face wreathed in smiles.

'Mrs Sugden! Your baby's out of danger!'

'What?'

We could hardly believe it. We'd nerved ourselves for the worst so often, because we'd seen other parents coming, white-faced, away from the children's wards.

'Jackie is being sent back to the cottage hospital. He just needs nursing along for another day or two. Everything is all right.'

'You mean – you mean he's cured?'

'He never had polio-myelitis! It's a strange illness –there are many things that seem to mimic the symptoms. He was certainly quite ill, no one denies that, but it was some lesser infection. Last night he showed at last that he had taken a decided turn for the better and this morning his temperature is quite normal.'

Nurse Grimsdyke was as pleased as we were, I believe. She beamed at us and led us to a little side ward where Jack was lying in a cot, kicking and waving his fists about. I realised it was the first time for twenty days that I'd been able to hear his voice. He was making a little sound I knew well – a sort of burble which meant he was awake but not unhappy.

I rushed to the cot and put my hands under him. Then I drew back, looking at Nurse in alarm. She laughed. 'Pick him up,' she said. 'It's all right.'

I can't tell you what it meant to me to be allowed to hold my baby again.

We were very, very lucky. Our little son was given back to us, unharmed. When, a few days later, I took him home from the cottage hospital, my heart went out to the mothers who had to brace themselves to spend years with a paralysed child or, the worst of all, for an empty place in the family. I remember talking about this to Mr Rosewell, our vicar.

'I don't understand why God allows it to happen,' I murmured. 'I know it says in the Bible that the sins of the fathers shall be visited upon the children but somehow it never seems right.'

'My dear girl,' he said, shaking his head at me. 'Do you really think God – the God of love – would harm a child?'

'Then how can it happen?'

'The sins of the fathers . . . That doesn't just mean stealing from other people, or doing deceitful things. There are sins of neglect, sins of carelessness. If this society really cared about its children, Annie, they wouldn't allow them to live in ramshackle old houses without proper sanitation. *That's* the sin which causes children to be sick.' He looked at me with great seriousness. 'It seems to me that God wants us to change things like that. I'm not one of those who believe that suffering is a "judgement" on us. In a way, you could say that the men who fought this war for us are showing they feel the same because they wanted to improve everything when they got back to Civvy Street. Perhaps the day will come when God's will really will be done, and we'll care enought for each other to see there are no slums, no malnutrition.'

We talked for a long time. The things he said made a great impression on me. As a result, while you could never call me a red hot reformer, I've always held to the belief that we ought to work for the improvement of our world. I'll admit there's not much one person can do, but with a few like-minded people it's amazing what an effect you can have. Easier in a small community like Beckindale, I agree – but even in great cities I know there are groups working all the time for the betterment of their surroundings.

Of course there are times when I get discouraged. I've seen some silly things going on around me and thought: 'With money like that, we could have given seaside holidays to a hundred children!'

The Groundnut Scheme, for instance. Do you remember the Groundnut Scheme? If my memory serves me right, the irrepressible Jack Train used to call the people involved with it the 'Nut Army.' Just after the war, some idiot in the Ministry of Overseas Development put forward the idea that a huge area of Tanganyika should be cleared of bush and planted with groundnuts –to you and me, that means peanuts. From this we were going to get gallons of cheap oil and tons of materials for making margarine.

Among my whole circle of acquaintances, I never heard a single person speak of it as a good idea. I think we all knew that it was nonsense. But somehow the money was spent and the machinery was taken out to Tanganyika. I noted in my diary: 'Cost, eight million pounds' with four exclamation marks.

Well might I exclaim. The machinery rusted and got broken among the intractable tree roots. The crop failed. When they harvested some groundnuts in the end, they got back two thousand tons for the *four* thousand they had planted.

Think of all the money that was thrown away before at last they admitted defeat. Think, too, of all the money that's spent tearing down the centre of an old town and putting up buildings that everybody hates. Think of the rows of friendly little houses that are replaced by great barrack-like 'housing estates' where people get ill with loneliness and worry.

It all comes back to what Mr Rosewell was talking about. God gave us brains and energy – we must use them properly, not on vainglorious schemes but on the simple things that make life better on a human scale.

A great thinker called Carlyle once said: 'Do the duty which lies nearest thee, which thou knowest to be a duty!' Mr Rosewell quoted it once in a sermon and I made a note of it in my diary. It's not a bad piece of advice to anyone who wants to do something to improve society. And to me, one of the duties that lie near us is to care for our children. To me, children are the hope of the future; they *are* the future.

I always think that I began to feel like this the day I took home my son from the hospital, grateful beyond words that he'd been restored to me.

3

CHAPTER THREE

I'VE SPOKEN QUITE a lot about Mr Rosewell, and that's probably because he retired from the ministry in the spring of the following year. It may seem a funny thing to say, but Beckindale was never the same after he left. It's true the Verneys were still at the Hall, but with the going of Mr Rosewell, something seemed to change in Beckindale.

He'd been a sort of mainspring to our community for as long as I could remember. He was quite old fashioned. He believed in a personal God and a personal Heaven. He knew everyone in Beckindale personally, knew their fathers and mothers before them. Nor was he slow to take them up when they did something wrong! Everybody in Beckindale was affected by his approaching retirement and I think I'm right in saying that ninety nine point nine per cent of the people were sorry about it.

Unfortunately, my husband Jacob was one of the point

one per cent who didn't care whether Mr Rosewell stayed or went. His attitude was the cause of the first real disagreement we'd had in our marriage.

The people of Beckindale took up a collection to make a presentation to Mr Rosewell. It was to be a silver rose bowl, which we thought was appropriate because of his name and because he loved the vicarage garden so much. We'd asked the cost of the bowl and having it engraved with a message from the parish. It was going to be quite expensive.

Jacob simply refused to make a contribution.

'I've no reason to be grateful to him,' he muttered when I tried to point out what a lot we had to thank Mr Rosewell for. 'He's often been right starchy wi' me –'

'Well, lad, when you were young you know you were a bit of a . . .'

'I'm not talking about that! Happen he felt he had to tick me off about going out o' nights, taking a hare or a pheasant. But now I'm a married man, wi' a farm o' my own, I expect to be treated wi' a bit o' respect – and Vicar allus spoke to me as if I were a nobody.'

'That's not true, Jacob. He might show a bit of disapproval now and again –'

'Who's he, to approve or disapprove? I can lead my own life–'

'But Jacob, Mr Rosewell's t'vicar! It's his duty to speak to anybody he thinks is falling short –'

'Aye, well, then, I don't "approve" o' that! I don't think any man has the right to speak down to me. And I'm certainly not giving money or putting my name to a message that will let him think I agree with his attitude. As far as I'm concerned, Mr Rosewell can leave Beckindale and good riddance!'

I was terribly taken aback. I'd no idea Jacob resented the vicar so much. It's extraordinary how you can live in the same house with a man, spend all your time with him, love him and feel concern for him, and yet not really know him.

I simply couldn't understand how anyone would feel dislike for the vicar. Even when he had to reprove a parishioner, it was always done with understanding. He never made a public show of his disapproval, he just went quietly to the 'offender' and had a word. True, there were some folk he wasted his time on – Jerry Crustock, for instance, who was well known to have contacts among the 'spivs' of Leeds and Bradford and who offered things for sale that he couldn't have come by honestly. And there was Marlene Hopps, now just coming up to seventeen years old, who certainly wanted to paint the dale red and wasn't going to be stopped no matter who lectured her.

But in the main, the people of the parish listened to the vicar and tried to live according to the precepts he preached. I'm afraid I'd taken it for granted that Jacob belonged to this majority.

Now that I found he didn't, I was in a predicament. Because of course I wanted our family to make a donation towards the cost of the rose bowl.

My father, too, was aghast when he heard Jacob's view. 'Now then, lad,' he said to him, 'that's no way to take on! Even if from time to time you disagree with Mr Rosewell – and I don't say I'm always completely with him, particularly when he preaches sermons about getting too partisan over cricket and bowls –' He paused. 'Where was I?'

'You were going to tell me I ought to respect the cloth, I think,' Jacob replied in a hard tone. 'And I'm damned if I see why! It's the man that matters, not the cloth. And if you want my opinion, Rosewell's an interfering old busybody.'

Dad and I drew in a breath. Those words were so disrespectful that we just didn't know what to say. We were all in the farm kitchen at the time, settling down for the evening. Dad was sitting in the straightbacked wooden chair he liked, with his seed catalogues. I was collecting socks and darning wool for a session with the mending. Jacob had some papers in front of him.

I realise now, looking back, that he was probably doing the farm accounts in preparation to filling in his income tax form. That was only too likely to make him tetchy. Our income tax was only about fifty pounds in all – that seems a tiny amount compared with what people pay today, but to us it was a lot, about one-tenth of our income for which Jacob worked terribly hard. He was trying to put money into improving the farm and found it a continual struggle to spare even small amounts for tools like spades and pliers. He had a long-term project to improve the drainage – after the floods he'd made a vow he was going to make sure the water shifted from his fields with more efficiency – but he couldn't afford the cost of the pantiles for the drainage channels. He must have been feeling very depressed and frustrated at that moment.

Dad said: 'I never thought to hear my own son-in-law say a thing like that about our parish priest. I'm ashamed of you, Jacob.'

'Please yourself. I'm still not going to give any money to his going-away present.

'Annie, are you going to let Emmerdale Farm be the only farm in the district that doesn't make a contribution?'

'What d'you mean, is she going to "let" it be like that? I'm the head of this household. I'm making no contribution to Rosewell's silver bowl.'

'All right then, I'll put the money I was planning to put in as from the Pearsons – but I'll say it's from Emmerdale.'

'You will not!'

'Are you saying you want to make a public demonstration of the fact that you don't like t'vicar?'

'I'm saying it's not your place to take on as head of this household. This is *my* farm. I'll say whether we're contributing from this house.'

Dad got up, put his catalogues under his arm, and made for the door. 'I'll go up to my room,' he said.

'Nay, Dad, it's perishing up there. Stay by the fire –'

'I'll put my overcoat on,' he said. 'I'd rather sit upstairs in my overcoat than be by the fire and listen to talk like this.'

I looked pleadingly at Jacob, but Jacob said nowt. My father stamped out and upstairs. There was a silence in the kitchen. Then I gathered my courage.

'Jacob.'

'Aye?'

'You said it was up to you whether there was a contribution from this house.'

'So it is.'

'I can't agree. I want to give money on my own behalf, to show I respect Mr Rosewell.'

'Money? What money? Don't expect me to give you any!'

'Nay, lad,' I sighed. 'I've got a pound or two that was given to me to buy something for Jackie when he's older – I'll give that.'

'You will not! That money belongs to my lad! You're not giving it to that old hypocrite's present!'

'Hey-up, Jacob! Whatever you want to say against t'vicar, you can't say he's a hypocrite!'

'I do say that! Yattering on about helping t'poor, t'refugees left over after t'war, and living in style in that big house –'

'That's not his choice, Jacob. The house goes wi' the job–'

'I don't notice that he's ever offered a home to any of them refugees! Plenty of room at t'vicarage –'

'Jacob, he's an old man! He's not up to coping with a group of strangers, some on 'em not even speaking English. And what would t'village have said, any road, if he'd invited a group of refugees?'

'Well, he never even suggested it, did he? And he's always on about giving up things during Lent and rubbish like that, but I see he gets books and magazine delivered from Harrogate, that must cost a fortune.'

'Nay, Jacob,' I said helplessly. 'You're seeing the mote in t'vicar's eye but forgetting the beam in your own –'

'What beam? What great crime am I guilty of, then? Are you going to say I don't do my duty as I ought? Don't I work all the hours that God sends, and more besides? Don't I plan and plot to make this a better farm?'

'Jacob, Jacob! I'm not accusing you of anything like that!' The whole thing seemed to be getting away from me, and I didn't know how. I couldn't understand what we were quarrelling about, to tell the truth. It didn't seem to be about Mr Rosewell, really.

I think he could see I was right upset, for he held his tongue.

After a bit I said, 'Listen, lad. For some reason I don't fathom, you've taken against Mr Rosewell. But you must allow me to go on thinking highly of him, for he's been a friend to me all my life.'

He grunted. I took that to be agreement.

'I want to give something to his present,' I went on, nerving myself for another outburst of disagreement. 'All right, happen I shouldn't give the money put by for Jackie. I want your permission, then, to give the money from the eggs for one week.'

The egg money is by tradition the property of the farmer's wife. Ever since we settled down together, it had been accepted that in my case that money went straight into the farm's finances. I waited, holding my breath, for my husband to say I had no right to ask such a thing. If that happened, I felt I was going to have to defy him. And I didn't want to do that. He was, after all, the head of the house. That's always been the way of things in the dales.

He sat for a while, pushing the papers about on the kitchen table and trying to think of what to say. I feel sure he regretted his outburst but didn't know how to retract what he'd said. I sat looking at his dark profile. The lamplight gleamed on his black hair and caught the glint of his dark eyes. He looked angry and stubborn and unhappy.

I got up and put my hand on his shoulder. 'Eh, lad, let's not have an ill thing between us,' I begged. 'Let me give the money. You'd let me knit a jersey to give to a friend you didn't care about. You'd let me make a cream cheese to give to a sick neighbour. Let me give a few shilling to Mr Rosewell's present.'

For a minute I felt the appeal was going to be wasted. Then he looked up and put one of his hands up over mine. 'Ah, lass, thas a winning way when tha wants!' he sighed.

So I gave a week's egg money to Mr Rosewell's silver bowl. I took pleasure in thinking that I was included among those who were mentioned in the engraved message: 'From his affectionate and grateful parishioners . . .'

That scene with my husband worried me every time it came back into my mind. It might just seem, on the surface, to be an argument about an old man whom we didn't really know very well. You might say that a vicar is to some extent cut off from the ordinary folk in his parish by the mere fact that he's a man of God; people feel they can't speak their minds in front of him.

But there had been so much resentment in my husband's tone. He seemed to be annoyed by the mere fact that Mr Rosewell had a big house and spent money on books – which we certainly couldn't afford to do, especially when we had a good travelling library from which to borrow them.

I think I sensed that he felt Mr Rosewell had things easy. That was what he had against him.

When men were demobbed after the war, I think there was a sort of points system to see who went first. Jacob came quite high because he'd volunteered for the Navy before hostilities broke out and also he was a farmer – he probably gained points because he was going back to help grow essential foodstuffs for the country. I have a feeling that Jacob had boasted a bit to his shipmates about his farm and what he was going to do.

I know he had high hopes, which were constantly brought to nothing, at first by his father. After Mr Sugden's death, he'd probably felt his way was clear. But those two years had been the worst for farming in our district that anyone could remember. What had been the use of putting his gratuity into electrifying the byre? The electricity supply broke down almost at once because of shortage of fuel to the power stations, and damage due to floods. The loss of stock, the cost of repairs . . . Everything seemed to have conspired against him.

But, you might say, it was just as bad for everybody else. So it was. That was what worried me. I found it strange that

Jacob should be almost blaming people like Mr Rosewell for being a bit better off. Not that Mr Rosewell was by any means rich! I think he was quite poor, really – but of course he did get his vicarage rent free and he didn't have to work with his hands from day's dawning till day's end. To Jacob, it seemed Mr Rosewell didn't really work. And so he was grudging about him.

He never mentioned again the matter of the presentation to Mr Rosewell. When Dad would insist on chatting about it – hoping to make him feel ashamed, I suppose – he held his tongue. He didn't come to the little ceremony at which we gave the silver bowl to the vicar, but then I didn't expect him to. I was a little bit worried that he might forbid me to write to Mr Rosewell, which to my surprise and pleasure he'd asked me to do – but no, he simply paid no heed to that. I kept up a correspondence with our former parish priest until he died at last in the home of his niece, aged eight-one.

That year was a bad one in many ways. We had another dose of 'austerity'. Sir Stafford Cripps had become Chancellor of the Exchequer and he made a very good broadcast explaining why Britain had to tighten her belt yet again, and posters came out on the hoardings begging us for 'ten per cent more!' in production. I'm sure we at Emmerdale would have been delighted to give him ten per cent more if only we could, but with only Molly to help Jacob and the intermittent assistance of my father, the farm couldn't really do much better.

That was the year the Olympics were held in London, at Wembley. I'm sure it won't surprise anyone to hear that I'm not much interested in athletics, but my menfolk were, and they got gloomier and gloomier as the events succeeded one another. I've got written down in my diary, 'I wish these blessed Olympics were over, everybody is so depressed!' I noted the events in which British athletes did well; happen I missed some, because it seems a bit scanty . . . We got a second place in the relay race and the marathon. Could that really be all? There may be other things, but I just forgot to make a note of them.

Any road, the newspapers and the commentators on radio kept on about how our wartime diet was to blame, that we were all under-nourished compared with the American athletes. I suppose that means that the Americans won all the events? I think they did. Now I come to put my mind to it, I believe the Americans took thirty-eight medals. Dear me, no wonder the men of Beckindale were so fed up.

Just after the Olympics, another minor disaster struck us. It seems so absurd now that I look back and wonder how it could have had such an effect. The fact of the matter is, cigarettes disappeared from the shops. In those days, there was no campaign against smoking. The stastistics about lung cancer hadn't been worked out then, and no one thought of disapproving of smokers the way they do now. Almost every man I knew smoked cigarettes or a pipe. My father smoked a pipe; he gave it up because of his chest cough, at the insistence of Dr Scott, not so very long ago. Jacob was a cigarette man; he'd learned to depend on them in the forces during the war, when it was an accepted thing to take a break in the middle of a training session for a ten-minute smoke. In fact, Jacob seemed to imply that smoking was positively encouraged.

The producers of cigarettes explained the shortage by saying that the visitors who had come for the Olympic Games had bought them all up. I don't really know if that was the cause of the shortage. All I know is that, in a place like Beckindale, supplies were almost non-existent. You might be able to get them by queuing up outside a tobacconist in a big town, but in the villages there were none to be had. The only way the smokers of Beckindale could get a packet was by kind permission of the wily Jerry Crustock, who seemed to know all the spivs in Leeds.

The word spiv has more or less fallen out of use. It was on everybody's tongue then. I don't know where we got the word from. Some folk said it was from the letters 'VIPS' backwards – VIP meaning 'Very Important Persons.' Others said it came from the schoolboy slangword 'spiffing', meaning smart or worthwhile. A spiv was a man who knew his way around the restrictions, who could always get anything that was scarce – bananas, nylon stockings, and now, of course, cigarettes.

The new vicar disapproved of Jerry Crustock even more than Mr Rosewell had done. His name was Antony Harper, his first name being the one he preferred to be called by. He was a complete change from Mr Rosewell. He was very informal, very go ahead – he believed in 'democracy' and didn't like to take any decision without having the opinion and approval of his parishioners.

To tell the truth, the parish found him a bit of a handful. He would preach fiery sermons about politics – and naturally his politics weren't the same as everybody in his congregation. He had strong views about the United Nations and the dock strike and the war in Malaya and Palestine. He shocked a lot of folk, I think.

You'd have thought, since Jacob found Mr Rosewell high-handed and autocratic, that he'd like the new vicar. Nothing of the sort! The first time they came face to face after the formal greeting at his first service, Mr Harper found my husband pulling the celophane off a packet of cigarettes.

'Ah!' he said with a frown. 'Been consorting with our black market agent, Mr Crustock, I take it.'

Naturally Jacob was annoyed. 'What if I have?' he countered. 'Can't get cigarettes any other way.'

'Mr Sugden,' said the vicar, 'there are people in refugee camps all over Europe who can't get cigarettes – or a home, or a job, or any hope for the future. The money you gave to Jerry Crustock for those cigarettes would have been better spent sending aid to them.'

'I'll spend my money how I choose, thank you!' Jacob retorted, and came stamping home in a fury.

Well, I have to admit I felt Mr Harper had been tactless, and often was. But he was young – I think he was only two years older than I was myself, and he'd had a different kind of life. He was full of high ideals and was very clever – I mean, he really had a fine brain. He went on afterwards to write books about political and moral problems. But happen he wasn't the best vicar for Beckindale.

I liked him, though. I liked his forthrightness. He had spoken out very strongly about the Berlin Airlift when some folks were saying we ought not to antagonise the Russians by supporting the Berliners – who, after all, said some, had been our enemies only a few years ago. The Berlin Airlift, if you remember, was when the Russians tried to cut off essential supplies from the city by closing the roads with tanks and armed forces. Britain and America flew in food and even water, I believe, for months. They just would not let the city become part of the Russian-dominated zone. I'm not able to say whether Berlin ought to be part of East Germany or not, but what I do know is that the citizens didn't seem to want that, and we owed it to them to let them live under the government they chose.

So when Mr Harper harangued the faint-hearted from his pulpit, I couldn't help agreeing with him. But at my side, my husband was fuming. 'Damn nonsense,' he muttered. 'It's nowt to do wi' us! All that money being spent on planes to go back and forth . . . Money down the drain, is that! The Russians will get the place, whatever they do.'

In fact, they didn't. I think early the following year, they reopened the road link. But that's by the way. The point is that Mr Harper was the sort of man who had Christian opinions and made no bones about stating them. And my husband wasn't the only person who didn't like that.

But despite these various defects, that year wasn't all bad. The weather was kinder. Although Jacob had a lot of bills to pay, he actually came out a little ahead on the money side. Yet he had a bad blow in the spring of the following year. He lost Molly Pepwith.

Molly had become so much a part of the establishment that we'd begun to think she would always be there. But the government were slowly disbanding the various wartime services, and the next that had to go was the Women's Land Army. It was due to be mustered out in the autumn of that year but Molly was one of those who was being released early. She'd been courting a local fellow, Les Upworth, for nearly a year, and they were emigrating to Australia.

I may say in passing that an awful lot of folk applied to emigrate in those days! Life was so hard in Britain that the prospect of a sunny life in Australia or New Zealand seemed very attractive. So Les had applied and been accepted by Australia House, and Molly was getting married and going with him. How on earth she was going to manage as a housewife in the outback I couldn't image. She was one of those who can't heat water in a saucepan without burning it. When she did her own mending, it was of the kind that looked as if it was accomplished with a redhot needle and a burning thread –it only held for about two days. But all the same, she was leaving us, and her place couldn't be easily filled, for she was willing and strong even if she often had to be carefully supervised.

She was to be married from her home in Leicester. We gave her a farewell party and I made her a present of a good cookery book. She wrote to me later from Alice Springs to say that none of the recipes in it were the least use out there, because it was so hot and dry that nobody wanted steamed suet puddings! I still get Christmas cards from her.

But her going made life very difficult for Jacob and my father. They split the work between them as best they could, but you know, after a hard day on Mr Verney's estate, Dad didn't have the same energy for the chores at Emmerdale. I had to pitch in.

You may be thinking, why didn't they hire a man? Well, we couldn't really afford it. Land Girls came at a subsidised rate, but a labourer would have to be paid the official minimum wage. Moreover, most male farmworkers expected a cottage. And we didn't have a cottage to offer. If we got anyone, he would have to live in with us, as Molly had done. But the fact was that most men wanted a place of their own, because most of those looking for jobs away from their own homes were married men, hoping to solve their housing problem by getting a tied cottage.

The housing shortage was really acute. It's still rumbling on, isn't it? But in those days it was dreadful. Agonised appeals were published in the advertisement columns of the newspapers. The newspapers were snapped up the moment they came out – in fact, I heard of people bribing newsagents to let them have copies before they opened their shops, so that the purchaser would have just that much start on everybody else in applying for a flat.

I remember seeing, in the paper's personal column, 'Grateful thanks to St Jude for two-roomed flat obtained after much prayer.' St Jude, you know, is the patron saint of lost causes. And some time about then, Jacob took me to the pantomime with our Jack, and one of the jokes was about the housing situation. The principal boy, the dame, and somebody else were in a competition to see who could tell the biggest lie. The other two told some fantastic tale – I forget what. The principal boy strolled to the front of the stage, brushed back her hair from under her Prince Charming hat, and said: 'Well, I know where there's a flat to let!' There was a roar from the audience, and the principal boy won the biggest-lie contest.

So for these various reasons, we couldn't get any help on the farm. We just managed to struggle on from day to day. I got to the stage where I longed for a chance to sit down and listen to the radio, without having to worry about the next piece of work waiting to be done. All the same, I knew I had a lot to be grateful for – I don't think I ever made the mistake of thinking I had any real hardship compared, for instance, with the refugees for whom Mr Harper kept on making appeals.

Then, late one evening, Jacob was brought home in a neighbour's car. He'd been in a scuffle in the Woolpack – and dislocated his shoulder.

CHAPTER FOUR

WHY WAS JACOB in a pub fight? Well may you ask! It was over politics — and if there was one thing Jacob didn't bother about, it was politics.

On the night he was brought home, I couldn't get much sense out of him. He'd had a bit to drink and wasn't too clear about anything. He said he had a 'sore back' so I helped him get to bed, a bit vexed with him for coming home in that condition and for waking our Jack.

Next morning, my husband couldn't get his arm into his shirt and was obviously in pain. Dad and I did the milking, then I got Jacob dressed somehow and took him by bus to Hotten to see the doctor.

Dr Anstruther came stamping out of his surgery to me where I was sitting anxiously in the waiting-room. 'What's that husband of yours been up to?' he barked. 'Wrestling with Man-Mountain Dean?'

I'd no idea who Man-Mountain Dean was, but I got the general idea. 'He had a bit of a disagreement with someone last night –'

'Ha! What's the other feller like, then? Damn fool.'

'Is it serious, then, doctor?' I ventured.

'Serious enough. He's got a compound dislocation of the scapula – that's the shoulder-blade – and though I *could* reduce it myself, I'd rather he went to the hospital to have it done. They'll have to strap him up. There's a lot of damage to the ligature. It'll be some time before he can use his right arm again, Mrs Sugden.'

My heart sank. 'Some time? How long, doctor?'

'Ten days, three weeks . . . I don't know. Depends what the ligaments are like. I can tell you this, you can feel the sogginess in the tissues when you just touch the area . . . What on *earth* did he think he was doing?'

'I don't know, doctor,' I said miserably. 'Is he going by ambulance?'

'No, no, no need for that. I'm going to Bradford myself later, when surgery's over. I'll take him.'

'But coming back –?'

'He can use the bus or the train. Good God, Mrs Sugden, he's still got the use of his legs and one arm – let him get about and make the best of it! I'm not wasting public funds on sending him by ambulance!'

With that he went marching back to his patient. By and by Jacob came out, looking rather white and very depressed.

'I'm sorry, love,' he muttered.

'So long as you're going to be all right . . .'

'But I shouldn't ever have let this happen.'

'Let's not talk about that. Jacob, will you be all right if I leave you? I've got to get back.'

I'd left our Jack with Mrs Towers at Beckindale Post Office. She was a dear good soul but she couldn't be expected to attend to a lively toddler and keep up with the demands of the customers at the Post Office. Besides, Dad would be coming home for his dinner soon. He could always get himself something to eat, of course, but he'd be anxious if I wasn't there, knowing I'd gone to the doctor's with Jacob.

'Yes, you get off home,' Jacob said. 'There's nothing you can do, really, is there?'

'Are you sure you'll be able to get back all right?'

'I'll manage.'

'Have you got money for the train fare and everything?'

'Don't *fuss*, Annie.'

'I'm sorry. It's just – I'm a bit put about – you're sure you're going to be all right?'

'Oh, yes, yes, get off home, for goodness sake.'

I think he was angry and embarrassed at what had happened. And well he might be, for I heard the story from Amos Brearley after I'd collected Jack from Mrs Towers.

Amos nipped out of the Woolpack to ask if Jacob was all right. I explained he'd had to go to hospital to have the shoulder put back. He groaned and shook his head.

'I tried to stop them, Mrs Sugden, really I did!'

'But what happened?'

'Well, they got into an argument, him and Arnie Groomes. About t'election.'

'About the election?' I was staggered. Jacob hadn't been the least bit interested in the election, which had taken place the previous week. He was fed up with the Labour Party, which had been in power and, in his opinion, made a grim mess of everything. He wouldn't vote for the Conservatives because the candidate was a friend of Mr Verney's and Jacob disapproved of Mr Verney because he had a lot of money (comparatively speaking) and because Dad was always quoting his farming views to him. In fact, Jacob hadn't even bothered to vote.

I said as much to Amos. He ran a hand through his already thinning hair. 'It were about Mr Tingwell,' he said.

Ah. That began to make sense. Mr Tingwell was a candidate for the Liberal Party – or, no, wait a minute, did he stand for that party called Common Wealth? Anyhow, he lost his deposit. What made him interesting to our village

4

was that the vicar was strongly in his favour and went out campaigning for him.

'Seems like your Jacob was taunting Arnie about how Mr Harper's candidate did so bad,' Amos explained, 'and Arnie got angry and began criticising your Jacob for one thing and another. They began exchanging remarks like –' He broke off, trying to remember some that he could relate to me, but decided none were fit for my ears. 'Well, remarks,' he went on. 'I asked them to be so good as to stop, because I don't allow that kind of thing in my bar, and Arnie was prepared to drop it, but I'm sorry to say Jacob said Arnie was glad of an excuse to stop because he was losing the argument, and . . .and . . . next thing I knew they were rolling on the floor. On my premises!'

I didn't know whether to laugh or cry at this story. It was all so idiotic. Jacob didn't really care a hoot about Mr Tingwell losing his deposit. But sometimes he'd get this devil on his shoulder and just have to make a quarrel –and this was how it had ended.

Jackie began announcing that he wanted his dinner so I thanked Amos and hurried off. The walk back to Emmerdale seemed to go on forever as I trudged through the drizzle of that day in early March. I hadn't realised how tired I was – and it still wasn't dinner time! Of course I'd had a disturbed and anxious night over Jacob, and then out to do the milking, and then the trip to Hotten and back . . . But it was a long time since I'd felt so weary and depressed.

Dad was already indoors. He was bustling about getting himself some bread and cheese and pickle. I said: 'Let be. That's not enough for a man on a cold day. I'll do you a grilled chop.'

'Nay, lass that's for Sunday dinner –'

'I'll make a vegetable and egg pie for Sunday. You have a chop now – it's t'quickest thing I can manage.'

Dad sat down to give Jack his dinner while I grilled the chop. Our Jack was always easy to please where food was concerned; he tucked into chopped cheese and bread-and-butter fingers, chattering away in his funny language to his

Grandad. It was the most cheerful thing about the house that day, I can tell you.

'How'll we manage, Annie?' Dad asked when I'd reported the news to him.

'We'll just have to do the essentials and leave everything else.'

'I'll take time off from Verney's. That'll be best.'

'Nay, Dad, you're needed there – and what about your wages?'

'Mr Verney'll let me have it as my holidays.'

'In March? Oh, Dad . . .'

'Never mind about that. It doesn't matter when I take it. I never go anywhere, any road.'

This was true enough. So Dad took his week's holiday with the permission of Mr Verney and we struggled on, the pair of us, to keep things going. Jacob did what he could, one-handed, but he was so unused to having only his left arm available that he kept fumbling things or knocking them over. Dad blurted out: 'Oh, let be, lad! You're only making things worse!' when they were trying to get feed put out to the cows. Jacob came indoors to me with a face like thunder. And in a way, you couldn't blame him. It's terrible to feel useless.

One day everything seemed to go worse than usual. Dad was worn out. Jacob was in a state of furious ill-temper. Our Jack had been playing up – unsettled by the atmosphere, happen. I stole a moment to go away and try to have a think.

I went to the old mill, which was a sort of refuge for me. I seldom had the time to go and sit there, but today I went in because I just had to get away for a bit.

And I'm ashamed to say I had a little weep.

It was just self-pity, I'm afraid. Poor me, I was saying to myself. The fact was, I still had a lot to be thankful for – my father was there to help us, I wasn't alone, and if only Jacob's pride hadn't been involved we could have asked for help from our neighbours. They'd have rushed to offer help. But he'd brushed off the first approach, from old Mr Jamieson, and naturally folk weren't going to lay themselves open to rebuff.

I was sitting there feeling sorry for myself when I heard a trundling noise and the beat of an old car engine. I got up and reaching the door, looked out. I couldn't see the car, because there was a screen of elder bushes by the mill which even though not in leaf made a barrier to a view of the lane.

A voice called: 'You there, Annie Sugden?'

I knew that voice. It was old Grannie Lee, the Romany. I came out of the mill to find her clambering down from the lorry that was her home.

Grannie Lee had been around ever since I could remember. It was said she'd had eleven children and forty-four grandchildren, but the only offspring I ever actually knew were her youngest daughter, Rosemary, who went off to make a fortune as an astrologer for a magazine, and her son Barnabas, known as Gippo.

Gippo was with her. He came from the other side of their van. This was an old-fashioned, high-built affair, with panels of sycamore and walnut edged with maple, all beautifully varnished. The cab of the lorry was painted a brilliant blue with taradiddles of yellow and red. Inside the lorry was fitted up as two rooms: a sitting room with crocheted antimacassars over the backs of chairs and ornate china ornaments held in place by brass rails, and the room Gran used as her bedroom. Gippo slept in a lean-to they erected at the side of the lorry wherever they stopped.

Lots of folk weren't best pleased when Gran and Gippo appeared in the neighbourhood. They said Gippo was lightfingered. Happen they were right. I can only say that nothing ever went missing from my mother's house at any time, although she was always quick to welcome Grannie Lee. And in all the time that Gran stayed on our land at Emmerdale, we never had anything taken. Perhaps it depends to some extent on how you treat people . . .

'Eeh, lass, I hear you're in a state,' she said, nodding at me knowingly.

'Trust you to know everything that's going on,' I said, summoning a smile.

'That man of yours got himself in trouble again, has he?'

'He's hurt his shoulder.'

'Aye, and can't be doing the farm work.' Gran approached the mill. 'Can I come in?'

I stood aside to let her enter. She glanced about, with disapproval. She sniffed. 'Could do with a tidy up in here, couldn't it?'

She was always the picture of neatness herself. She had hair black as a raven's wing except for one or two wiry threads of silver. She wore it in two plaited 'earphones' at either side of her head, parted neatly down the middle so that it came away from her brow in two dark wings. She wore golden 'keeper' earrings. Her eyes were black as boot buttons. She had a wrinkled face, but it was strangely youthful all the same. She was usually clad in a pleated tweed skirt and a sweater and boots — I mean men's boots, the kind that have leather laces and stop at the ankle. They were always highly polished; she made Gippo clean them every day and shine them with a toothbrush.

'It isn't used now,' I said. 'I just came here to have a think.'

'About how to manage, eh?' She dusted an old box with her handkerchief and gingerly sat down. 'I thought you could probably do with a helping hand, so here I am.'

'How d'you mean, here you are?'

'Don't you want to hire me, then?'

'Grannie! I hadn't heard tell of you for months until you showed up a minute ago. Besides, it would be up to my husband if he took you on.'

'I don't see where he's got much choice,' she said, pleased with herself. 'From what I'm told, he's landed himself in a right old mess. Me and Barnabas, we'll put everything to rights. Just you persuade your man to give us a place to park our van, and a little bit o'cash for the food rations from the grocer's, and so long as you provide us with fresh eggs and home-baked bread and that, we'll be happy to help you out.'

I wasn't so sure that Jacob would take them. He was

touchy about Romany travellers. Folk were apt to say to him, 'I see your cousins are in the neighbourhood again, Jacob.' This was a reference to the old story that his great-grandmother was supposed to have been a gipsy girl, from whom he was supposed to have inherited his dark good looks. It's true that when you saw Jacob and Gippo together there really was a resemblance, although Gippo was smaller and thinner.

I took Gran back to the farmhouse. To cut a long story short, Jacob struck a bargain with them. They were to stay for the foreseeable future on conditions that were really very advantageous to us, from the money point of view.

I think Gran was getting tired of journeying about the North of England. I believe I've mentioned already that the gipsies are still quite a force in the Appleby area, but for most of the year they move about. Gran must have been about seventy, and had never had a settled home – not that she'd want one, she was happy with her van. But I suppose the war had been hard on her, with Home Guards continually stopping her and wanting to know what she was up to, and identity cards always being demanded by the police and so on. I really don't know how she got the petrol to run that van, you know. It was still on ration, and I can't believe, though I never inquired, that any special allowance was made to Romanies! Of course, during the war, she had a horse-van. It was only after horse-drawn vehicles began to get a bit awkward on the main roads that she bought a motorised van.

All I can say is, it was one of the best days in my life when Gran settled down on Emmerdale land and set about giving me a hand. She was a tower of strength. She'd turn up before milking every day, and either help with that or take on some other task. Our Jack took to her in a minute. The first time she stepped into our kitchen, he walked towards her with both arms held out as if he'd known her all his little life.

She was a wonder with the washing. She knew how to get clothes clean with all sorts of natural things that she brought in from the hedgerows. She'd get stains out with fullers's earth, she'd make a marvellous starch for printed cotton curtains out of potato flour which she collected by steeping cut potatoes in cold water and scraping the residue from the bottom of the bowl. The great thing was, you could then cook the potatoes!

I wasn't so keen on her cooking, but there's no doubt she had a wonderful knowledge of what was edible among the growing things. She'd bring in all kinds of mushrooms, at all times of year: 'There's allus a mushroom growing if you know where to look,' she'd say. She found a medlar tree that I didn't even know existed, although I thought I knew the countryside well around Beckindale; it was in a sheltered nook not far from the ruins of the old abbey. I suppose it was brought there centuries ago by some monk from the Mediterranean, and how it survived I'll never understand. Medlars are a rare treat, though they have to be half-perished before you can eat them. I used to bake them, like apples, and serve them with a touch of redcurrant jelly.

Gran decided I didn't have enough baskets for laundry and shopping, so she just sat down and made me some. She had withes in her van, that she'd cut from willows she'd passed on her travels. There's a willow called the common basket osier, which is pollarded – that's to say, constantly cut back to the trunk so that lots of twigs will grow. These are the twigs that are used to make baskets; I've found a lot of people believe that they only grow in places like Spain or Italy, but you can see pollarded osiers (salix viminalis) on the banks of many streams in this country. Of course, they're generally on somebody's land. You can't just go trudging along and cut the osiers without permission. Incidentally, the word osier, which we use for a willow suitable for basket twigs, comes from an old Medieval word for a willow bed. A willow bed was where the peasants grew willows for the purpose of basket-making.

It was from Gran that I learned to wash my baskets regularly in soap and water. It keeps them supple and they last for ages. If you've brought back an expensive 'souvenir' from the Mediterranean you might like to give it an occasional scrub to keep it in good condition! This is true for those basketwork ornaments you see on people's mantelpieces, too.

You ought to have seen me and Gran doing the spring cleaning. I had no electricity, you see, so I couldn't have an electric cleaner. We used brooms and feather dusters. We'd move all the furniture to the centre of the room and cover it with an old sheet. Then we'd sprinkle old tea leaves on the floor — I never threw out tea-leaves, because I used them to 'bank up' the fire. But when I had cleaning in mind, I'd put the tea-leaves by for several days, then rinse them several times in a colander under running water to get the tannin out of them. These were tossed down, damp, on the floor and the rugs, to keep down the dust as we swept. *Then*, they were brushed up into the dustpan and wrapped in newspaper and put on the fire to keep it in at night – waste not, want not.

I didn't have any fitted carpets. I had rugs and runners. These were taken out, hung on the washline, and beaten with a carpet-beater made from withes — a beautiful thing, really, with a long twisted handle and a 'palm' like a cloverleaf, quite ornately plaited.

We made the windows sparkle by cleaning them with powdered whiting. This was made from chalk, which we 'precipitated' by scraping into muslin and then hanging in a jug of tepid water. After about an hour, all the powdered whiting had filtered down to the bottom of the jug and the grit and little scraps of stone had stayed in the muslin. I recommend whiting to anyone who can still get hold of it – windows are never brighter than when they've been cleaned this way. You just rub the moist whiting over the panes, let them dry, then rub it off with a washleather. Cheaper than stuff you buy in a bottle and, I think, much the same thing!

In those days we didn't have all the preparations in tubes and aerosols to clean our belongings, biological powders to bring about magical disappearance of stains. I used to wash tea and coffee stains out with warm water to which I'd added a little glycerine. I got rid of egg – of which our Jack spilt a lot! – with benzine soap. Ink stains came out with lemon juice (if I had a lemon) or bought oxalic acid. I still use some of those old hints – for instance, if I have the bad luck to scorch something while I'm ironing, I still rub the mark with a stale crust of bread and nine times out of ten it clears it up.

I don't know how I would have managed without Gran. And Gippo was certainly a great help to Jacob. Gippo had a way with animals so he was marvellous when there was a calf due; his mere presence seemed to soothe the mother. He could espy a ewe in trouble from miles away. But he wasn't so good on the field work. He'd do it, but he seemed to mistrust our tractor. He was happier in the barn, sorting potatoes or repairing our tools with his nimble fingers.

What he liked best of all was to be out and about at night, when the rest of us were abed. I'm not saying he was always tickling trout or snaring a duck. I'm sure he spent hours watching badgers or following an otter in the beck. But the drawback was, he began to take Jacob with him.

My Jacob had always been a night owl. In his young days he'd led my brother Eddie astray by persuading him to wander abroad in the dark. I can't really explain why it was so attractive to him; I suppose there was a sort of magical freedom about it – the countryside looks different under the moon, and when you're out under the night sky no one expects you to be ploughing a furrow or picking beet.

Now and again he'd give me a rabbit he'd taken in a snare, or a hare. He never handed over a pheasant, although I sometimes smelt that unmistakeable savour coming from Gran's cooking-pot by her van.

'No good'll come of it,' my father would say, looking worried. 'He's a grown man, married, with a bairn to think on. What does he think he's up to?'

'It's just a restlessness, Dad,' I'd say. 'It'll pass.'

But it didn't. All through March, April, May and part of June of that year, he would be missing at night – I'd reach out my hand to see if he was there beside me and find the pillow cold, the space empty. He was out ranging over the dales with Gippo.

Next morning when I got up to give our Jack his morning rusk, I'd hear Jacob downstairs already. The milking would have been done, the two of them would be sitting over a pot of tea. There was a scent of open-air dampness about them, from the dew on their clothes. I'd look at Jacob, and think how little I understood him. There was a mysterious force that drew him away from his home out into the world where the owl drifted by, where the nightjar called, where the fox cantered through the fields with the starlight glinting on the silver tip of his tail.

Of course it had its effect on his daytime work. It took its toll. The rest of us had to shoulder the tasks he didn't get around to. I was nerving myself to speak to him about his midnight expeditions when something happened that cured him.

Another war broke out.

CHAPTER FIVE

IN A WAY, there had never been peace. Although the Second
World War was over, Britain had been involved in fighting
in many parts of the world. There had been the trouble in
Malaya, when guerillas tried to frighten the rubber planters
off their estates, and the unhappy situation in Palestine
where British soldiers were involved in keeping refugees
from landing.

Then I believe I'm right in saying that the French were
having trouble in what was then called Indo-China, and
there had been uprisings in Greece. But we in Britain were
taken up with our own troubles at home, so that when, for
instance, the Berlin Airlift ended we all sort of sank back
into apathy. Well, I ought to speak for myself, really,
oughtn't I? All I can say is I didn't think anything about it
when North Korea invaded South Korea.

The United Nations was supposed to be in charge of

getting a peace treaty in Korea. I don't know the ins and outs of it, but we all became aware that the North was Communist and the South was . . . well, non-Communist.

To tell the truth, I didn't even know where Korea was. I had to look it up in the atlas at Hotten Library. It turned out to be a big peninsula sticking out from the mainland of Asia across the sea from Japan. It was really interesting to look at it on the map. I sometimes think we don't realise how true it is that we're living in 'one world'. This unheard-of country was between China and Russia. Russia! It came as a shock to find that Russia was round that side of the world, that the port of Vladivostok, which I'd certainly heard of, and knew to be a place in Russia, was sitting across the water from Japan.

But I didn't go and look up Korea as soon as the war broke out there. I have to admit that I didn't take much notice. It seemed to have nothing to do with us. It was the kind of thing they were always going on about at the United Nations in New York, where one or other of the big nations would make a speech and propose a resolution and the other side would block it and nothing would happen.

But this time — I don't quite understand how, but it happened – the United States seemed to end up being the champion of South Korea. I can't for the life of me remember what the North Koreans were supposed to be after when they invaded the south . : . Anyhow, the capital fell to the Communist forces at the end of June, only a few days after the invasion.

The Americans landed troops and a real war began. Still I don't think I was paying much attention. Nor was anyone else I talked to. Then the names of British regiments began to be mentioned on the radio bulletins – The Argyll and Sutherland Highlanders, I think, and the Middlesex Regiment.

In our house, we only began to sit up and take notice when Jacob heard the British Navy mentioned. He waved the rest of us to stop talking and turned up the radio. 'That's my old ship!' he said. It seemed the British Far

Eastern Fleet had been in action.

Jacob had been in the Far East during the war – had been stationed in Ceylon. Of course he was interested to hear mention of his old ship, which still had men serving that he used to know.

We must have been right thick. It still didn't come home to us that Jacob might be involved. We didn't wake up until my husband got a letter in a manilla envelope with OHMS on it. 'More tax, I suppose,' Dad teased as he opened it.

Jacob nodded, thinking he was right. Then he gave an exclamation of astonishment and dismay. 'Hey-up! I've been recalled to my ship!'

Well, I don't know if any words can convey the shock we felt.

I forget all the details now. It seems that when the men in the Forces were demobbed at the end of World War II, some were put on a list which meant they could be recalled to active service again if hostilities broke out. You must realise that Britain still had a call-up at that time. Young men were called up for National Service – and you still hear folk these days saying it would do youngsters the world of good to have that happen to them now. 'It would make a man of him,' you hear them say about some lad that's be-having badly.

But it seems to me quite wrong to take a young father and husband away from his home against his will, except in times of national emergency. Our trouble was, we hadn't understood there was any kind of emergency. We hadn't realised that Korea was going to have any importance in our lives.

There was a paper among the others in the envelope saying that if Jacob's circumstances had changed since he was mustered out of the Navy, he could appeal against his recall. He filled in the form and sent it in at once, and we waited in some suspense to hear the result. He got a tele-gram telling him to present himself before a Board in Port-smouth. Portsmouth! That was right the other end of the country and would mean Jacob would be gone from home for a couple of days.

There was no expense involved, mind you. He got a travel warrant and he was to put up in naval barracks and all that. But it meant we'd be short-handed while he was gone.

As to what we'd do if he had to go back into the Navy, I didn't even let myself think. Well, that's not true. It kept going through my head, but I kept saying to myself, 'Nay, no good can come of getting in a fret.' But if he was actually recalled, we were going to be faced with three choices. My father would have to give up his job with Verney's and take on Emmerdale; we'd have to hire a man to run the farm; or we'd have to give up.

I couldn't manage on my own with only Gippo to help me. Gippo had a lot of talent in some ways, but he was unreliable. Gran would have taken on the household chores all right, and that would have left me free to see to the stock and the fields, but there are some things a woman hasn't the physical strength for. Besides, I'd never yet learned to drive a tractor. I knew very well that the men of Beckindale weren't going to let me have the use of the tractor we all shared. There had to be a man on the farm who could undertake things like that.

Jacob set off for Portsmouth in his demob suit, which was still his best suit. He went on the Tuesday, to report before the Board on the Wednesday morning. If all went well, he would be back on the Thursday. What I mean is, he'd be back anyhow – they weren't going to snatch him straight on to a ship, like in the old days of the press gang! My meaning is that if there were no delays such as going for a medical or anything like that, he'd be back on the Thursday.

We didn't have the telephone at Emmerdale so he couldn't ring us to let us know what had happened. We'd have to wait until he got back in person.

Dad was pale with anxiety about it all. He'd made up his mind to hand in his notice to Mr Verney the minute he heard Jacob was going back to his ship – but he didn't to do it. The newspapers – which we now read with much more attention – seemed to be saying the war in Korea was as good as over. This was September, and the North Koreans had retreated back across the Naktong River. Seems funny to me now when I write down that name; I copied it out of my diary, and before Jacob got that letter I'd never heard of the Naktong River nor knew how to spell it! But now the Naktong River was important. If British troops were over there chasing the North Koreans back behind their own frontier, what did the Navy need my husband for?

So you see, Dad felt that if Jacob was recalled to his ship, he'd likely be back in Beckindale again within a couple of months. And if Dad had given up his job at Verney's to run Emmerdale during that time, he wasn't going to get his job back just because Jacob was demobbed again. If he gave up his job, he'd lost it for good, he felt.

I think now that he was wrong. I think Mr Verney would have taken him back if he had had to leave. Dad was a marvellous man with stock. Mr Verney knew his worth. But all the same, when a man's getting towards fifty he doesn't want to put himself out of a job. It might not be so easy getting it back.

But he'd made up his mind to do it. He didn't say so, but I could sense it. While Jacob was away, he went right off his food. He hardly ate a morsel. Our Jack kept ticking him off about it: 'Eat up, Grandad, or Ma will be cross with you!' For of course, our Jack was expected to clean his plate like a good little boy.

Gran said to me: 'Lass, don't thee suffer. I'll not let thee down, never fear. As for Gippo, granted he's not the best farmhand in t'world, but he's got good in him, has Gippo. We'll manage atween us if your husband's took.'

She was looking on the bright side, and I was grateful to her. But she knew, as I did, that Gippo's good resolutions would only last for a week or ten days. He'd be up and about early and late for a while, but then he'd get bored with work and feel the urge to go roaming off. I didn't hold it against him; it was the way he was. Yet it was no help to Emmerdale to have a hand like that as our mainstay.

Of course the neighbours would help. Old Mr Jamieson

was always ready to lend a hand. He farmed a small place that ran along our north border, which he worked with the help of only his wife Maud. They were a stalwart old pair. Then there was Peter Rekstow at Goldstone – he'd come in and do what he could.

But they had their own land to care for. True, harvest was over and a slight lull would come over the countryside during the next few months, but what if we had a bad winter? What if the weather turned against us again? Then there was the problem of Jacob's plans. He'd wanted to increase the dairy herd by ten cows in the coming spring but what ought we to do if he was in the Navy? Abandon all his projects? It wouldn't be fair to expect our neighbours to help us expand at the expense of their own work.

I'm sure Dad had all these ideas going round and round inside his own head. Neither of us mentioned them; to each other we kept up a front of being quite calm and sensible. But there must have been a difference in the feeling of the house, for our Jack kept pulling at my apron and saying: 'Ma, what's the matter? Ma, why is everything so quiet?' And of course: 'Ma, where's Dad?'

Those three days seemed to go on for ever. By Thursday evening, when we expected Jacob back on the bus from Hotten after his trip from the south, we were on tenterhooks.

But he didn't appear.

I'd gone down to meet the bus. There were five passengers, but my husband wasn't one of them.

I felt myself going cold with apprehension, for it seemed certain that he'd been kept in Portsmouth for reasons to do with the recall. I couldn't believe he'd lost his appeal; if they could take a man who was working a farm with almost no help, contributing to the food supply of the country . . . well, it seemed daft to me! Yet he hadn't turned up.

I hung about, thinking he might have missed one of the connections on his journey. He might have got a lift from somebody. But in those days there weren't as many cars about as there are now, and after about half an hour I gave up – only one car and two lorries had gone through Beckindale, and none of them had stopped.

Dad had walked out to meet me in the lane by the time I set out for home. 'What's happened?' he called.

'I don't know, Dad. He wasn't on the bus.'

He took my arm through his and walked with me back towards the house. It was past dusk, and the place looked welcoming with the glow of the lamplight in our window.

'Dont thee be set down, Annie lass,' he murmured. 'He'll just have missed a train somewhere, I s'pose. He'll be here in t'morning.'

He didn't come in the morning. Nor in the afternoon. Nor in the evening. By this time I couldn't conceal the fact that I was dreadfully worried. I couldn't understand why we hadn't had *some* notification. I decided that next morning first thing, I was going to the police cottage to ask Constable Lyle to make some sort of inquiry for us.

Saturday morning, then, as soon as the milking was over, I pulled on my coat and set off for the police cottage. I was climbing the stile to take the short cut across the back lane when old Mr Jamieson came hurrying across the corner of the field.

'Mrs Sugden! Mrs Sugden! Thy Jacob's walking up the front lane!'

'What?' I was so surprised and delighted that I turned without thinking and actually fell off the stile. Mr Jamieson came rushing to help me up, and made ineffectual attempts to clean the mud off the side of my coat and skirt.

'Never mind, Mr Jamieson, never mind – I'll see to it when I get home.' I scrambled up and ran off, calling, 'Thank you!' over my shoulder.

Jacob had just come indoors when I got there. He looked such A stranger in the townified suit he'd put on to go before the Board. I hesitated just inside the kitchen door, staring at him.

'Well, here I am!' he said, laughing with a flash of his white teeth. 'Home to stay!'

I'm not often demonstrative, but I must say there was a

5

bit of a scene then. I threw my arms round him, and our Jack grabbed one of his legs, and old Gran was in the background clapping and cheering . . .

I sent Gippo to take word to my father, who of course had gone to work at Verney's. Then I set about cooking a breakfast for Jacob, who was explaining what had happened at the interview and was very animated about his feelings at seeing Portsmouth again.

Gran, very tactfully, took little Jack out for a walk. Jacob told me what the officers had asked and how he'd answered and how, really, it had all been a bit of a formality. He'd been in and out within half an hour.

After a bit, having gone through it several times, I said, 'Then what happened about coming back? We expected you the night before last.'

'Oh, that . . . Well, yes . . . That's right.' Some of my husband's good spirits seemed to fade. 'Well, you know . . . Since I was in Portsmouth and had time to kill before the train, I thought I might just as well look up some of my old shipmates . . .'

'You what?'

'It seemed silly to rush straight back. I had some good times with those lads, Annie.'

'You went to see your friends?' I said, feeling a funny choking feeling in my throat. 'But that could only have taken a couple of hours, Jacob.'

'Nay, then, y'see . . . Tom took me to see Alf, and we thought we'd have a bit of a reunion . . .'

'Jacob!'

'It only seemed fair, Annie. They wanted to buy me a drink so I had to stand my round, didn't I?'

'But you . . . you're *thirty-six* hours late!'

He turned his head away from me. 'Well, it got out of hand, a bit.'

'Got out of hand?'

'I meant to catch the train after the one I'd told you about. But I missed that. And then the connections wouldn't have been any good, so I stayed over until the next morning . . .'

'But you've never been travelling since yesterday morning – twenty-four hours, to get to Beckindale?'

'Nay, well, y'see, – they asked me to go out to Gosport to see Bert Higgins — he's in the Stores Depot there –'

I sat across the kitchen table staring at my husband. 'Are you telling me,' I said at last, 'that you went drinking with your friends instead of catching the train home to us?'

'Well, Annie, it was difficult to say no –'

'When you knew we were on tenterhooks about what was to happen here at Emmerdale?'

'Oh, it was good news I was bringing. I knew that would make up for everything.'

I don't know when I've been so angry. I was right put out. I felt he'd been thoughtless and unkind. For the sake of having a good time with his old shipmates, he'd put us through two nights and a day of the most tremendous anxiety. I thought he'd had an accident, or been hauled straight on to a ship heading for Korea, or something.

I couldn't bring myself to speak. I just got up and took off my apron and pulled on my muddy coat and walked out.

As always when I was in distress, I went to the old mill. I walked to and fro in its dusty interior, trying to settle my mind. I was still too angry to cry or say anything aloud.

But anger fades, and good sense comes back. You know what it says in Proverbs: 'He that is slow to anger is better than the mighty; and he that ruleth his spirit than he that taketh a city.'

I had to go back to the house. I had the midday meal to prepare. I had a little boy to look after. I couldn't sit here feeling outraged and sorry for myself.

When I got back I found that Jacob had changed his clothes and gone about his work. That was a help; it gave me a bit longer to be in control of my words when I spoke to him again. I wanted to avoid breaking out into reproach. As I thought it over I realised that Jacob had found the temptation to enjoy himself just too much for him, and perhaps he wasn't to be blamed. Life at Emmerdale was very hard. He saw very few people except the neighbours and the friends of the Woolpack. Who could blame him for falling victim to the longing to sit about with friends of his wartime days, exchanging yarns about the past?

My father came in for his dinner. Naturally he wanted to hear all about Jacob's trip, so I told him the result of the Board and all that side of it. 'So why was he delayed, then?' he asked.

I took a slow breath. 'He stayed over to see some of his old friends,' I said.

'He what?' I saw his face go red with ire. 'Well, now, if that isn't –'

'Dad,' I broke in, 'I want you to keep off the subject with Jacob. I don't want any trouble.'

'Trouble? I'll give him trouble –'

'No, that's just what I want to avoid. Dad . . . what's done is done. It'll do no good going over it and making him feel guilty –'

'But hang it, lass! He ought to feel guilty!'

'Well, I think he does. I think he . . . Well, never mind. I've been thinking, and I feel it's wrong of us to expect him to live his life just the way we want him to. He's not a slave, Dad! He's got a right to a couple of days off!'

'But not without letting us – letting *you* — know!'

'Never mind about that. It's in the past already. He's back, and he's not going in the Navy. We ought to be celebrating, not talking about how badly he's behaved.'

'Look here, Annie, you've got to make a protest o' some sort. He's no right to treat you like that! He was as good as missing, wi' never a thought about how you felt –'

'I don't want to talk about it. And I don't want you to talk about it, Dad.'

'I'm not going to let it go by –'

'Dad,' I said, 'I hate to have to say this, but you're living in Jacob's house. It's not for you to say how Jacob should behave.'

'Annie!' He was aghast. 'I never thought to hear you say a thing like that to me.'

'I don't want to. Believe me, I don't enjoy it. But this is Jacob's house. You're not to reprove him for his actions. Is that understood?'

'But how are you ever going to sort him out if you don't speak to him when he's done wrong?'

'I don't know that I'm thinking of "sorting him out",' I said with a sigh. 'Jacob's a grown man. It's not up to me to change him.'

'But somebody's got to –'

'Don't you recall the saying, Dad? 'A man that's changed against his will is of the same opinion still'. The more you talk at Jacob, the more you'll make him stick to his view that he hasn't done anything wrong – and I don't know that he has, really.'

'You're just being soft because you don't want a row –'

'Happen that's the reason,' I agreed. 'Tell me what good it'll be to have a row?'

'Well, it'll bring Jacob to his senses! I mean, before he went for this thing in Portsmouth, there was all that business of creeping out at night to poach pheasants and things. He's hardly ever twelve to the dozen in the daytime, Annie, and you know it.'

'Either he's got sense enough to see that for himself, or it's a waste of time to point it out.'

'If you ask my opinion –'

'I wasn't, Dad. I'm sorry to speak to you this way, but the fact is, this is atween me and Jacob. I don't want your opinion.'

'Annie!'

I could hear the sound of Jacob walking across the yard towards the door. I said warningly to my father, 'Now remember – no rebukes or remarks.'

'I don't know that I agree with that –'

'If you start trouble with my husband, Dad, I'll walk out that door until you fall quiet again.'

This stopped the words on his lips, I could see. He sat staring at me, perplexed and unhappy but silent. When Jacob came in there was a strange atmosphere but he wasn't met with angry words.

Granny Lee came in with little Jack a little later. I served the food. Jack prattled on about the berries he'd seen on the trees by the beck, and Gran's scheme to pick some autumn twigs and preserve them with glycerine. Beech leaves are best for this, but any leaves that colour up in the autumn can be kept in their glowing tints by standing them in a vase containing glycerine and water; you leave them to drink up the water and some of the glycerine, and when the water is gone the leaves are 'preserved'.

Hardly anyone else spoke except Jack. Gran had of course gone to cook Gippo's dinner by their van. Jacob talked to Jack, and Jack talked to Jacob, and that was the extent of the conversation. When the meal was over, Jacob went out again to get on with his work. He and Gippo did the evening milking without coming in for afternoon tea. After the evening meal, Jacob settled down by the fire, across the hearthrug from my father.

'Not going to the Woolpack?' Dad asked pointedly.

'No, it's nice to be home.'

'Had enough drinking for the moment, is that it?'

I frowned at Dad, but Jacob didn't rise to the taunt.

'Aye, happen that's it,' he agreed.

That night when we were getting ready for bed he suddenly said to me: 'Aren't you going to say anything?'

'About what?'

'About me being late?'

'Nay, lad.'

'But you were angry, Annie. I could see you were.'

'So I was.'

'But you aren't any more?'

I set down my hairbrush. 'Jacob,' said I, 'let's not talk on that topic. I'm just grateful you're back to look after the farm.'

He was sitting on the end of the bed, his elbows on his knees, staring at the floor. 'Looking after the farm,' he repeated. 'It's funny, Annie. When you come back again after being right away, you suddenly see all the things that want doing.'

'There's always things to do on a farm.'

'Aye, but I've not been doing 'em. And you've not reproached me. I don't think many women would have been so forebearing, love.'

I made no reply. To tell the truth, I never thought of myself as 'forebearing'. It's just that I don't see the point of bursting out into a lot of angry words. What is it the poet says: 'Three things cannot be recalled, the spoken word, the moment past, the lost opportunity . . .' If folk were less eager to rush into speech, a lot less damage might be done.

Jacob got up and came to put his arm round me as I sat in front of the old dressing-table mirror. He looked at me through the reflection. 'I'll change, love,' he said. 'I'll try to be a better husband. I've realised what a lot I nearly had to give up, when I got my papers.'

'Good for thee, lad.'

'I mean it, Annie. I promise to keep my mind on Emmerdale.'

I nodded at him.'

'You believe me, don't you?'

'Aye, of course I do.'

We were very close at that moment. I don't quite know why it should have been so after the strange anger I'd felt against him that very same morning. Happen it was because we'd both kept quiet and given ourselves time to think that we hadn't had a quarrel, and happen it was the relief of not having a quarrel that made us feel so at one with each other.

CHAPTER SIX

JACOB KEPT HIS promise to the best of his ability. Even my
father, who was on the alert to find fault, had to admit that
in the next few months his son-in-law was a model farmer.
He was up early and late, working with a will. He hardly
ever went anywhere except to market. He stopped spending
so much time in the Woolpack.

'Anything up wi' your husband, Mrs Sugden?' Amos
Brearley asked me at the end of about three weeks during
which Jacob had only bought two separate pints in his bar.

'Not a thing.'

'I only wondered, 'cos he don't seem to come in much
these days.'

'He's busy, Amos.'

'So're other folk,' mumbled Amos, 'but they don't give
up their pleasures.'

Another pleasure Jacob had certainly given up was the

jaunts over the countryside at night with Gippo. Old Gran said to me, 'Gippo's quite put out wi' thee! He's lost his night-owl companion.'

'So much the better, Gran.'

'I dunno,' she muttered. 'Gippo's likely to get into even more mischief if he's out on his own!'

I couldn't regret the changes that had come about, because it gave me more of Jacob's companionship when I needed it most. I was expecting my second child, which somehow this time seemed to drag me down in my health. I don't know whether it was the hard work I'd been doing on the farm, or the anxiety I'd had, or what. Whatever the reason, while I was expecting our Peggy, I was quite poorly.

By this time the National Health Service was supposed to be in full swing but they still hadn't got enough maternity beds, so only mothers of first babies and those who weren't expected to have straightforward confinements were scheduled to go into hospital. I was fixed up again to have the services of Nurse Spenlow, who kept dropping in to see me and looking a bit dubious.

'I dunno,' she said. 'Happen you should go into hospital this time . . .'

'But why? We managed fine last time.'

'But you were in better health then.'

'I'm fine, Miss Spenlow. It's just that I'm tired.'

'And why wouldn't you be!' she burst out. 'Working all the time, never getting a rest in the afternoon like I keep telling you –'

'Oh, you know I can't go upstairs and drop asleep, Nurse! First of all there's our Jack –'

'That little old gipsy can look after him for you, Mrs Sugden. He seems happy enough with her.'

'But there's the chores to do. It's not easy to –'

'Let the chores go hang! They'll be here when you're gone, my dear.'

But it's no use telling a Yorkshirewoman to let the chores go. In any case, it isn't fair to ask a man to accept scratch meals when he's done a hard day in bad weather. He needs something hot and substantial. I couldn't expect my husband or my father to eat bread and cheese because I was 'resting' on my bed.

Grannie Lee took charge unexpectedly. She came bustling in one morning to find me sitting breathless on a kitchen chair, having just had a funny turn when I was sweeping the floor.

'That's enough!' she said, taking the broom out of my hand. 'You're going to behave from now on! I'm going to do the housework and cook the meals. The men'll have to divide your outdoor jobs among themselves –'

'But, Gran –'

'Not a word out o' thee! You're getting paler and thinner every day except for your middle, I'm going to be the housewife from now on.'

I knew she didn't really relish the role, because she liked to spend a good part of each day out of doors and she also liked her snug little van. Another point was that though she was an excellent cook in some ways, both Jacob and my father preferred my dishes to hers. Then I was sure that either of the two men would mishandle the geese and the poultry; geese are very odd creatures, you know, who get attached to one particular person. I had an old gander who was almost like a dog; he'd follow me round the yard and push his beak into my apron to let me know he was there.

But I had to submit. I really felt under the weather. The result was that, with all the cosseting I got, I picked up again and was able to have the baby at home after all instead of being taken into hospital. Mind you, I didn't have quite such an easy time as with our Jack, but that's neither here nor there. I was as happy as a lark when Nurse Spenlow put a squalling bundle of flannelette blanket and scarlet-tinged baby into my arms. That was our Peggy – just like her to make her entry into the world with as much fuss as possible.

She continued to be a bit of a problem. She wasn't an easy baby. I often think that it was about this time that our Jack began to be a bit of a problem too. I really didn't have as much time to spend with him as formerly, and I think he tried to get consolation by being with his daddy. But Jacob hadn't much patience with little ones. He didn't like having our Jack under his feet. So the poor little chap felt very much pushed out of the centre of attention.

These days mothers are solemnly lectured about not letting their elder children have their noses put out of joint when the younger children arrive. I don't think anyone ever talked to me on that point, but I didn't need telling, really. It was easy to see Jack was naughtier than he used to be so he ought to be played with and chatted to. But it's one thing to know what's wrong; it's another thing to have the time to put it right. Try as I might, I just couldn't give our Jack all the fussing he seemed to need.

Perhaps that's why, as he grew older, he grew away from us. But it may simply be that he was always a bit of a loner. Our Jack wasn't like the other lads in the neighbourhood. I don't know why . . . I don't think there was ever anything I could have done to change him, and happen I didn't have the right to do so, in any case.

My main job at that time was to settle our new baby into her routine and get back to my household tasks. Haymaking was in progress so there was plenty of work to be done, with the food having to be taken out to the haymakers. Then there was a little bit of a lull before Jacob was called on to help with the grain harvests in the other farms, so he suggested we should go for a day out to Harrogate.

That was the year of the Festival of Britain. The main events were in London, of course; the newspapers were full of photographs of the Skylon and the Dome of Discovery on the South Bank, and there were broadcasts of the events from halls and theatres.

I remember one evening when we were listening to a concert on the radio and the batteries ran out. My father cast up his eyes and remarked: 'Dome o' Discovery! Age of Technology! And we haven't nobbut oil lamps – no electric to run our radio!'

'We'll get a new battery tomorrow,' Jacob promised.

We didn't forget to buy it in Harrogate. We did quite a

bit of shopping there, for the shops had a grand display of things and of course I'd got a little bit of money as presents to our Peggy.

Yorkshire had taken a share of the Festival of Britain activities, naturally, and Harrogate had all sorts of events going on, in the Hydro and the Assembly Rooms and so forth. I remember we went to hear 'Elijah', and then to an exhibition of paintings and sculpture by Yorkshire artists. We were looking at a stand with some watercolours of land-scapes when we met Emily Tewkesbury.

'I dunno who painted that,' Jacob was saying, 'but he's never actually seen lichen on a tree trunk or he'd know it's always on the north side.'

'Well, that's where it is,' said a voice from behind us.

'Nowt o't'sort,' Jacob said, turning round. 'If you look at them shadows, you see the sun's shining on the side of the tree where the lichen is. So it can't be north, can it? Sun don't shine from the north.'

The girl who'd spoken looked a bit put out. 'Oh dear,' she said. 'That's a real bloomer, isn't it.'

'Aye, but happen not many folk'd notice. He won't know.'

'The painter does know,' she said. 'It's me.'

'Who?'

'Me. I'm the one who painted that.'

Jacob coloured up at having spoken out of turn in her hearing, and I was embarrassed for her. 'No offence meant,' I said.

'None taken,' she said. 'I only wish I'd had someone like you to cast an eye over it before I put it on exhibition. I did the colourwork from pencil sketches, you see – separate sketches of the tree-trunk detail and so on. I've put them together all wrong, it seems.'

'You should come and take a look at the trees round where we live,' said I. 'We've got some grand old oaks on our land.'

She asked where we lived and we had a long chat. She was a nice girl, about of an age with myself but seeming younger because, I suppose, she was still able to please herself what she did with her life. She had straight brown hair hanging loose round an oval face, and though she wore bulky tweeds and thick-knit stockings, you could tell she was slender as a hazel twig. In a way there was something almost schoolgirlish about her.

I never thought to see her again, but a few weeks later there was a knock on the door, and there she was. 'Remember me?' she inquired. 'Emily Tewkesbury. You said I ought to come and look at your oak trees.'

'Come in, come in,' I exclaimed, delighted by her visit. 'Sit thee down. Would you like a cup of tea?'

'Oh, I would! It's *so* hot outside!'

It appeared she'd been roaming round on foot all day, carrying her easel. A prize had been instituted for the best painting of Yorkshire rural life, and she was looking for subjects to paint so as to enter for next year. I gathered she had to have a 'group' of paintings; it was all something to do with the Festival of Britain, somebody had given some money to further local talent.

While I was mashing the tea, Grannie Lee came in. You should have seen Emily's eyes light up. She watched the old gipsy woman like a hawk while she was with us, and after she'd gone bouncing out again she burst out: 'Who is she? Does she live nearby?'

'On our land, as a matter of fact.' I explained about Gran and her van. Emily was fascinated.

'I didn't know there were any gipsies still in existence,' she said. 'Is she the only one?'

'No indeed. She's got a son, Barnabas – known to us as Gippo and sometimes as Paderewski.'

'Paderewski?'

'Because he wears his hair long and is a bit of a musician! He makes and plays whistles.'

'Good lord! This is extraordinary! And you say they've got a caravan?'

'A motorised van – but it's quite special.' I poured more tea for her. 'But you know, if it's a typical scene you want, I don't know if gipsies really qualify. Romanies like Grannie Lee and Barnabas, they're quite rare. Most of the travelling folk are what the gipsies themselves call *didekei* or chancers – not true Romanies and not too honest, some of 'em. But they're more common on the roads than folk like Gran.'

'That doesn't matter,' she protested. 'There's so much character in that face of hers! I wonder if she'd let me paint her?'

I was doubtful. 'She never lets anyone photograph her. We've had picknickers here who've wanted to, and she always turns away. She thinks she'll get the evil eye if anyone takes her likeness, I think.'

'Oh, that's nonsense –'

'Not if she believes it,' I pointed out. I was a bit taken aback by her enthusiasm.

'Could you speak to her for me? Persuade her to sit for a portrait?'

'Well, I don't know that she's got the time –'

'She works for you, does she?'

'In a manner of speaking.'

'But you give her time off, of course.'

'Of course,' I agreed, a bit deadpan. I was trying to imagine myself keeping Gran's nose so much to the grindstone that she didn't have time off. A likely story!

'I'd promise to paint her in her spare time,' she went on. 'Could you explain to her that I think she'd make a marvellous subject for a portrait – a rural portrait? It might mean I'd win the prize for next year's exhibition, and that in its turn would mean I could spend another year studying.'

I must say I felt a bit of a stab of envy at that. Another year studying! As yet she hadn't had to shoulder any responsibility. But then I thought, 'But she hasn't got a beautiful little son and daughter.'

The long and short of it was that I promised to persuade Grannie Lee and perhaps Gippo to sit for Emily to paint. If I'd known how much trouble Emily was going to bring, happen I'd have taken care to fail in my persuasions.

Gran agreed surprisingly easily. I told her that she would

bring good luck to Emily and she couldn't resist the idea. So within a week Emily had taken up a room at The Feathers in Connelton and was driving daily to Emmerdale with her easel and case of tubes of paints; she was going to use oils this time, and was very keen.

Jacob found her almost unbelievable. That anyone could spend all day on 'doing painting' seemed incredible to him. He couldn't feel that it was work in his sense of the word, and so he began to drop in on Emily wherever she happened to have set up her easel, to see what she was up to.

What began out of idle curiosity began to be a real interest to him. Gran said to me one afternoon when she came in to fetch lemonade for the harvesters, 'That man of yours is in the coppice watching yon Emily doing a painting of a whitebeam.'

'Yes, he's quite intrigued.'

'Huh!' she grunted. 'If I were you I'd see her off the premises.'

'Gran!'

'Well, it's not right! He's spending far too much time watching her when he should be at work.'

'Now, Gran,' I scolded. 'That's just being silly.'

'Nowt o't'sort! He's a married man. He shouldn't be hanging around a bit of a girl like that.'

'You're reading something into it that isn't there.'

'No I'm not. Your Jacob is always on the lookout for something to take his mind up rather than his work! You take my advice and tell Miss Tewkesbury to be off.'

'I couldn't possibly do that.' What reason could I possibly give? After inviting the girl to come to our farm? Besides, it would be inhospitable beyond anything I'd ever thought of. In all my life, I'd never asked anyone to leave.

I put Gran's words out of my mind. I had other things to think of, as it happened. As a part of the celebrations for the Festival of Britain, our rural district council had arranged an outing for the children – they were going to a circus in Leeds.

Our Jack was going with the coach party, under the care

[79]

of the members of the Women's Institute. I had my hands full with him, for he was very excited. He'd just started Sunday School and some of his little friends were also going. He came home full of it.

'Sally Newsome is going to have a new dress,' he reported. 'And Willie Wyatt's getting a real blazer. Ma, can I have a blazer?'

He'd no idea what a blazer was, but he'd got the hint that his little friends would be turning up in their best clothes. Now, our Jack was always turned out neat and tidy, and suitably clad for the weather. But Jacob couldn't afford to deck his son out in the latest fashion and we certainly had never thought of buying a blazer for Jack! This was the era when children's clothing suddenly took off into a new range; up till then they'd been clad in little dresses and in short trousers, just as their parents had been in their childhood. But all of a sudden it was the fashion to dress children like little adults. Little bits of kiddies were being turned out like fashion plates. Little girls would have frocks that were to all intents and purposes small versions of what their mother was wearing, and the little boys wore long trousers and jackets to match.

There was no question of our Jack having anything like that. I was knitting him a new jersey, so I hurried to finish that. And I'd made him a smart little pair of shorts in grey flannel, cut down from a pair of his father's trousers but — if I do say so myself – neatly tailored. I always knit my menfolk's socks, so Jack had a pair of calf-length socks with coloured tops. To my way of thinking, he looked right smart.

We walked into Beckindale the morning of the outing, to put him on the coach. There was a coach from Hotten, going round the villages collecting up the passengers for the outing. I must say that when I saw the others, I was a bit staggered. Little Julia Stanforth had on a Vyella dress with lace edgings that made her look like a Victorian miss. Nancy Prior had a skirt and jacket – a costume, we once used to call it! – in tailored jersey with piping along the edges. Jimmy

Loxley was all got up in a dark blue suit – long trousers although he was only the same age as our Jack. Willie Wyatt was wearing the famous blazer, with a badge on the pocket and brass buttons, and moreover a striped tie – he looked like the captain of some cricket team, although he was only just five!

Little Jack was too excited to notice all this. He gave me a hug and clambered on the coach when Miss Deldison gave the command, and off they went.

All went well. He was safely delivered back to me that evening, half asleep, sticky with candy floss, grimy with circus dust. I put him straight to bed after just wiping his face and hands with a flannel. Next morning he was full of it: 'I went to the circus! I saw the clowns, and the effalents. Peggy didn't go, did she? She's too small. But I'm big, I went to the circus!'

On the Friday the Hotten *Courier* came out with a report of the outing, and a photograph. Normally we don't take the *Courier* but of course, because Jackie's photo was printed, we bought it. There they were, all the children from our area standing in front of the coach in Hotten. A laughing, smiling group, healthy-looking and happy.

Yet something about it gave me a pang. Most of the children were so smartly dressed. Only a couple were what you might call 'ordinary'. There was Joanie Maldon from Hemsingdon Farm, in a very sensible skirt and blouse, and Annabel Henderson in a dress that had clearly had the hem let down (and not very well at that). Among the boys, it was our Jack that stood out. There was something sort of home-made about his outfit. All the others were not only tidy, they were positively elegant or cute – but Jack looked as if he came from a home where they couldn't afford cuteness.

Well, too bad. It was nothing to be ashamed of, after all. Time was when parents would have thought shame to waste money on turning their children out looking 'fashionable'. It was good sense and good value that used to count, I told myself – but I was a bit sad all the same, that we couldn't afford to give our little lad a few of the things the other

6

children had.

Jacob didn't notice this point at all, luckily. He studied the photo and remarked: 'Looks like a little angel, doesn't he? Nobody'd guess what a limb of Satan he's turning into!'

'Jacob! He isn't!'

'Oh, you're too soft with him, love! He's getting to be a wayward little devil.'

'It's just a phase,' I defended him. 'It's because of the baby. It'll pass.'

'Humph,' said Jacob.

There were severe gales that autumn, that brought down one of the great old oaks on our land and took a lot of the slates off the barn. Jacob was up there on a ladder for days, making it rain-proof again. At the end of October there was another election but this time my husband didn't get into any arguments about it. Mr Churchill came back as Prime Minister. It was a funny feeling; having the wartime leader take over again made us think that everything would be different. I don't know in what way! It was just that we were all getting tired – exhausted, almost – with continual effort, continual austerity. Things didn't seem to go well for Britain no matter how hard we tried – and there were the casualties in Korea to underline the fact that World War II hadn't brought universal peace.

Then a most extraordinary, out-of-the-way thing happened in our village. It was only a little thing, really, but it had a tremendous effect on me.

The first I heard of it was when a young man drove up to our farm on a motor bike, announcing himself as a 'stringer' for the Hotten *Courier*. 'What are you going to get for your little boy from this Festival of Britain present?' he inquired.

'You what?' I exclaimed.

'Haven't you heard? Statheley's in Harrogate haven't rung you about it?'

'We're not on t'phone, lad.' He was drenched in his motor-bike gear – it was bucketing down. 'Come in and have a cup of coffee while you tell me what you're on about.'

The story as he explained it was this: some reader of the

Hotten *Courier* living abroad had seen the picture of the kiddies grouped in front of the coach that had brought them from Beckindale, and had sent instructions to one of the best stores in Harrogate the every child in that photo should have a new dress or suit or something of that kind.

'It seems he used to live in Beckindale,' this lad explained. 'He wants to take some part in the Festival of Britain and this is the way he's chosen to do it.'

'But who is it?' I demanded.

'Seems he wants to remain anonymous.'

'But – good gracious – he must be rolling in money! Outfitting those kids will cost a fortune!'

'Expense no object! I gather he's sent an open cheque to Statheley's.'

I was really staggered. I've heard of eccentric millionaires, but this really took the biscuit.

'So what are you going to get for your little boy, then?'

'I don't know. It's all such a surprise.'

I was in two minds whether we ought to accept. At first I was inclined to think of it as charity. But when I discovered that all the other mothers were going to take advantage of the opportunity, I began to change my mind. After all, the Priors could easily afford to pay for Nancy's clothes, and so could the Wyatts. Mrs Stanforth said to me: 'Julie's set her heart on a party dress for Christmas parties. I've seen just the very thing in Statheley's.' By and by it became clear that everybody else was going to choose something, so our Jack would be saying, 'Why can't *I* have something, like everybody else?'

Why not, indeed. According to the way the Hotten *Courier* put it: 'This exiled Beckindaler wants to show his attachment to his home village, no doubt, and we hail his sensible generosity in turning to the children of the district for his tribute to his native soil.'

Whatever you may think of the florid style of that, the sense behind it was convincing. So I took our Jack into Harrogate on the coach with the others that day, and we all chose an outfit for our child. I need hardly say I got a blazer and a pair of beautifully made long trousers for our Jack. He was so excited while he was trying them on that he was almost unmanageable. But then all the kiddies were the same — delighted and noisy.

The Women's Institute, who'd organised the original outing, had the list of the children who had to have a garment. While every name was being checked off by Miss Deldison and the head of the children's clothing department, I had a word with a nice young salesgirl.

'Don't they love it all,' she said to me, nodding at the children, many of whom were clutching their parcels to their chests.

'Yes, it's a great event for them. A sort of fairy tale present. Whoever this benefactor is, he must be a nice man.' I was struck by a thought. 'I suppose it *is* a man?'

'No way of knowing. It's all a most mysterious business. Our head buyer got this letter from a solicitor in Harrogate saying he'd had instructions to set all this in motion, and naturally our advertising department let the papers know at once. Pennies from heaven, it is, for the advertising department!'

'I'd have thought they'd try to keep it quiet. After all, it's what this man seems to want.'

'Well, we've gone along with the instructions to the letter. But that doesn't stop us being inquisitive! I really wish I knew who was behind it. I'd like to write and tell him about what today has been like – seeing all these happy faces . . .'

'Yes, wouldn't it be nice to write,' I agreed. 'Just to say thank you.'

'Clearly that's the last thing he wants. There's no clue to his address.' She leaned a little closer. 'Except – I did hear a rumour that the instructions about payment came through the London branch of an Argentinian bank.'

'What?'

'Argentina. That's in South America,' she explained.

I knew where Argentina was. It was the country to which Laurence Stanton had gone eventually when his ship was torpedoed during the war.

I don't believe I said another word all that afternoon. We all piled back on the coach and were taken back to Beckindale. I walked home with Jack; he was chattering away like a little monkey, and I don't think he noticed I wasn't answering him. When we got indoors, we had to have a fashion parade of the outfit I'd bought him: Jacob sniffed, Grannie Lee applauded, Emily Tewkesbury smiled and nodded.

'It's not a very practical outfit, is it?' my husband remarked.

'No . . . But just this once, Jacob, I thought I'd let the lad have what he wanted.'

'He gets too much of what he wants,' he replied. But nevertheless he was a bit proud that out Jack looked so smart in his new clothes.

I was too busy the rest of the day to give much thought to what I'd been told. But next morning, after I'd seen to the poultry and done the breakfasts and bathed and fed Peggy, I took our Jack for a walk, and somehow my footsteps led me to the old mill.

Jack would play quite happily in the garden gone wild at the back, safely hedged off from the millstream. I sat down on an old box, and let my mind wander.

Argentina . . . That was where Laurence was now.

Laurence Stanton – the boy I nearly ran away with during the war. Only my sense of duty – or perhaps my cowardice – prevented me from going with him to London, to keep out of the way of his parents until they'd sailed for America. In the end he went with them, and that was the last I saw of him for years. Nor did he write, and I sadly accepted that he'd forgotten me.

When Laurence reappeared that winter after I was married to Jacob and living at Emmerdale, he explained he'd been unable to write to me because he'd been so very ill due to exposure and injuries received when the ship was sunk in mid-Atlantic. It had taken him years to get fit enough to come back for me. He'd expected to find me still waiting for him.

I'd had to send him away, of course. I was a married woman, expecting my first baby. As far as I was concerned, that was the end of the matter – although I admit I often used to think of him. Not in any wrong way, you understand. But I used to wonder how he'd got on, whether he'd married and settled down in Montevideo.

His mother, who had also survived the wreck, had married a rich shipowner. Laurence had told me his stepfather had a good job lined up for him in the firm and I think he said he was to inherit the business.

And now, out of the blue, someone from Argentina had arranged for the children of Beckindale to be given this lovely present.

You may think I was imagining it all – that I got it all wrong – but somehow in my heart I knew that the instructions for that present had come from Laurence. And more than that. I knew he'd done it so as to give my little Jack an outfit to equal the best-dressed child in the photograph in the *Courier*.

Perhaps I was mistaken, but the way I worked it out that morning as I sat in the old mill was this: Laurence had arranged to have the local paper sent to him regularly – I suppose by airmail, for the action about contacting Statheley's had followed so close on the publishing of that photo. And it seemed to me that the only reason Laurence would have for reading the Hotten *Courier* was to keep track of what was happening at Emmerdale Farm.

I mean, what other reason could there be? Why would a busy executive of a shipping line bother to look at a little local rag? It could only be that he wanted to keep some slight contact with Emmerdale. The local paper in a district like ours is the repository of all the local activities: births, deaths, marriages, flower shows, agricultural news, market prices, church outings . . .

It sent a strange little shiver through me. Laurence had known about the birth of our Jack, about the birth of Peggy – because those were recorded in the Hotten *Courier*. I searched my mind for other items that might have mentioned

.Emmerdale.

The floods, the work of reconstruction that had gone on afterwards – Emmerdale had been noted as one of the farms that had suffered some damage. My father's flowers had won a prize in the Horticultural Show two years ago.

What is it that Gray says in that lovely poem of his: 'The short and simple annals of the poor'. That's what those little items are, really. The short and simple annals of the ordinary, I suppose you'd say – little events that are important to us but have no sway in the great tide of affairs.

Yet out there in a country thousands of miles across the Atlantic, Laurence Stanton was reading about us.

I felt strange about it. Perplexed, touched – and happy. I was happy that he still thought of me kindly.

There had been a time when we were all the world to each other, when we were very young. That was all over but it was comforting, it was gratifying, to feel that he still cared about me enough to keep in touch. He even wanted to help – oh, only in a small way, and without letting it be known he was involved. But for the gossip of that salesgirl, I'd never have connected Laurence with the present to the children of Beckindale. Yet now I knew. I had no evidence, really. I just *knew*.

I wouldn't mention it to anyone. Laurence wouldn't want that.

But from now on, no matter what happened, I'd always feel that a friend was thinking of me, keeping an eye on what concerned me. I knew Laurence and I would never see each other or even write to one another, but there was something good and helpful in the thought that I had such a faithful friend.

CHAPTER SEVEN

JACOB HAD A great plan in mind to improve Emmerdale Farm. The government had made an offer to farmers to provide money for the improvement of hill farms and marginal land – and Emmerdale had quite a few acres of hill slope in its boundaries.

The problem was, the farmer had to put up as much as he was asking from the government. In other words, the farmer had to have half the money needed for the work. Jacob didn't have that kind of sum, but he had hopes he'd get Mr Verney to advance it to him.

Perhaps I should explain here that we only rented the farm in those days. We owned the stock and the equipment, but the house and the land belonged to Verney Estates. At present things are different; Joe, Matt, Henry Wilks and myself are equal shareholders in Emmerdale Farm Limited. Now, if we want to do something, we can do it if a majority is in support and (of course) if we have the funds.

But while Jacob was alive, he was only a tenant farmer. If he wanted to alter the farm in some big way, he would have to have the approval of Mr Verney.

The 'Mr Verney' now was George Verney, who'd done so well in the war. He inherited when his father died in 1949. He was very like the old man in many ways: a very keen farmer, always on the alert for ways of improving his estate. He looked after his woodland, he bred champion cattle, he was a model employer.

Jacob knew that he'd get no argument from George Verney about reclaiming hill land and draining the marshy ground at the bottom of Blea Head. But he wanted to get more than agreement. He wanted to get money. Without that,. he wouldn't be given the government grant for improvement.

The day he was to have his interview with Mr Verney, he put on his good suit, which I'd pressed specially. In those days men still wore shirts with separate collars, and I'd starched and ironed his collar to a nicety. I must say, he looked very smart when he set off – a handsome lad, my Jacob.

'Wish me good luck,' he said as he went out of the yard.

'I do, lad, I do!' I called after him, waving.

'He's pinned all his hopes on that, hasn't he?' Grannie Lee remarked when I came indoors again.

'Aye, he's got his spirits high on that score.'

'I hope he's not heading for a disappointment.'

'Don't you think Mr Verney will put up the money, then?'

Gran shrugged. 'I dunno. I know nowt about money. You know us Romanies put no importance on it. But I saw a shadow over the window of your bedroom this morning. It's a disappointment coming, Mrs Sugden.'

'Oh, Gran . . .!'

'You know I'm always right when I see what's coming, love. You steel yourself. I have it in my mind that Mr Sugden's not going to get a good welcome from Mr.

Verney.'

She was right. Jacob came home two hours later with a face like thunder. He wouldn't talk to me about it, and went stalking out again as soon as the Woolpack opened that evening. All evening he sat in a corner, so Amos told me later, speaking not a word. When he came home he was a bit the worse for wear, and went straight to bed. So it wasn't until next day that I heard the ins and outs of it.

'Would you believe it? He's put in for a grant himself!'

'But then . . . that ought to mean he's all the more eager to help you get one.'

'Nay, lass – don't you understand? He has to put up half the money to get the other half off the government. So he's put all he can afford towards his own scheme. He's got far more land to work with than I have, now hasn't he? So he's put in for a bigger scheme. And it means he's got no money to spare to help me improve Emmerdale.'

'Oh, Jacob . . .'

'I tried to make him see that, since he owns Emmerdale, it would be to his advantage to lend me the money. He just kept saying, "Sorry, old chap, it just can't be done!" Old chap!' Jacob grimaced. 'Trying to make out he's a pal of mine! I tell you, it's always the same. One law for the rich and one for the poor.'

'But Mr Verney isn't exactly rich, Jacob –'

'And he's not exactly poor, either. Why should the likes of him get a grant to improve his land? He's got plenty that's in good fettle –'

'But the government just wants to increase the acreage of agricultural land, no matter who owns it –'

'Well, that's not fair! The money should go to them that really needs it –'

'That's true, lad, but in a way, it's logical to help Mr Verney. He's a very good farmer – he'll make good use of what he reclaims –'

'Meaning that I won't?' Jacob shouted. 'Are you telling me I don't know how to farm?'

'Nay, love, I'm not saying that at all –'

'Oh, I've heard your dad on about how I make mistakes. You pay too much heed to what he says –'

'That's not true, Jacob, I've always –'

'You've always compared what I've done with what your father talks about at Verney's. "Mr Verney this, Mr Verney that" – he's always quoting Verney at me. I'm fed up of it! And let me tell you, I know a damn sight more about it than George Verney ever will. Catch him getting his hands dirty mucking out the mistle, or up a ladder repairing a roof!'

It was no use talking to him when he was in a mood like that. He'd cut in on everything you tried to say, so that you never finished a sentence and he always got you on the wrong foot. I waited until his temper had died down and then suggested he might try for a loan from the bank.

But it was no good. He had nothing to put up as a guarantee. If the land had been his own, then the bank might have advanced the money. But not to a tenant farmer with such a small, a mediocre profit record – that was what they said to him.

He was terribly dejected about it. It was this feeling he had, that the money was there and he *deserved* it. He just couldn't raise the sum necessary to have his share of the pot of gold.

From then on, Jacob was very touchy about his abilities as a farmer. That remark about a 'poor profit record' had touched him on the raw. In his own eyes, he'd done his best, provided for his wife and family – what more could be expected of a man?

My father had long ago learned to curb his tongue and not offer advice to Jacob. Now he learned not to talk too much about Verney's. He'd watch Jacob and perhaps see something that could be done better in some new way but he didn't dare mention it.

'I'll tell thee summat, lass,' he said to me. 'His heart's not in it any more.'

'He's had a big disappointment, Dad.'

'All the more reason to set to and show what he can do. Hanging about the Woolpack isn't going to help.'

'That'll pass'.

'I hope so. And I hope the same about the time he wastes watching that Emily fiddling about with her tubes of paint.'

It was a fact that Jacob could often be found standing behind Emily studying what she was doing. During the winter she hadn't turned up so much, I'm thankful to say. It was too cold most of the time for her to handle a paintbrush easily.

In the February of that year, our king died. I think it had been expected, for he'd had at least one operation. Princess Elizabeth, as she then was, had gone off to Nairobi with Prince Philip but they were called back less than a week later. We had a queen to reign over us.

I still kept up my diary although not so regularly as when I was a single girl. I wrote in it: 'Now we begin a new Elizabethan age. I wonder if it will make a difference to everything to have a woman at the head of things.' And then, a bit I remembered from my history books: 'I know I have the body of a weak and feeble woman, but I have the heart and stomach of a king, and of a king of England too.' That was from a speech she made (I mean the first Queen Elizabeth) to the troops who were going to fight the Armada.

That's a thing we'd never say nowadays, is it – 'the body of a weak and feeble woman'. We've come to realise that women in some ways are as strong as men. They may not have such good muscles, but they have endurance, they survive better. I forget when it was, but there was a balloon attempt to cross the Atlantic from east to west (from Ireland to America) which ended in disaster. And it was the woman among the balloonists who survived.

That's not to say I believe women are superior to men. I can't go along with those noisy young women (and some not so young, who ought to have learned better) who want to prove that women are better at everything. It seems to me that the Almighty wouldn't have made men and women except for some good reason. 'Male and female created he them,' as the Good Book says. Each must have a role to play and why one side should try to look down on the other is a mystery.

The coming of the young princess to the throne caused a lot of discussion of woman's role, and chivalry, and matters of that kind. I found it very interesting. It seemed to me that most of the writers, or the broadcasters on the radio, had little experience of what women actually do. Women on a farm have an essential part to play; if you doubt that, just go and look at any farm that's run by men alone. The place always has a half-derelict look about it. Some women would set up a cry that farm-women only do the domestic chores. Well, what's wrong with that (if it were true)? Men who work long and hard on the land must be properly fed and cared for or they won't be able to carry on.

Here in the North, there's a tradition of women working. At the time I'm speaking of, it was still not quite usual throughout the country for a married woman to keep her job on, according to the pundits – but there have always been married women in the cotton mills and the tweed mills of the North. We have a hundred-and-fifty years' experience of the 'working housewife' so we're not so taken aback as some folk over the problems that follow. Happen it's because we're a down-to-earth, commonsensical sort of people, but we've managed all right with our womenfolk out at work; we haven't had hordes of delinquent children, or broken marriages.

I'm not saying it's easy. Life's never easy, is it?

But I can't help thinking that women's lib, as it's called nowadays, is asking too much. I had more respect for the old Suffragettes I used to read about in history class; they had dignity, and their aims were clear-cut. I know it can be said they were mostly well-off and were only interested in 'liberating' middle-class women, but what they began was bound to have an effect on all classes. These days, the 'liberators' want to make other women feel guilty if they don't share their ambitions. I think that's arrogant, really.

True liberty, true dignity, comes from feeling that you have value. Perhaps having a queen helped women to take a fresh look at themselves and realise their own value. I do recall that there was an impulse of hope, of optimism as she took up her duties. I think many women felt a kind of kinship with her; she was a mother herself, she upheld principles that most of us believed in.

Another thing I noted in my diary soon after the death of the king was 'Identity cards revoked!' The little cards with our identity registrations had to be carried all through the war, and it took eight years to see the last of them when the war was over. Eight years! And we *still* had food rationing!

However, there were good things to record in that year. The war in Korea seemed to be as good as over. There wasn't a peace – to tell the truth, I think they're still negotiating peace terms now! – but hostilities had died down more or less, and troops were being brought back.

This was how David Annersley came back to Beckindale. He was mustered out of the Army after being wounded near Panmunjon. I'd heard Dad say that David had reappeared but hadn't seen him until one day David drove up in the Verney's estate van.

'Hello, it's Annie, isn't it?' he said, leaning out of the driving seat as he came into the yard.

I was carrying the washing indoors. It was a blowy March day. My hair was all over the place and my eyes were watering from the dust blown into them.

'Er . . . David, is it?'

'Brought your Dad back to you,' he said, going round the other side and helping my father out.

Dad was a bit bent over. 'What's wrong?' I cried.

'Nowt to get in a state about, lass,' Dad replied crossly. 'I'll just get indoors and set me down. Thankee,' he added to David.

I hesitated. David said; 'He all right. A bit winded. A young horse Mr Verney's just bought knocked him over. Mr Verney thought he ought to go home and lie down for the rest of the day.'

'Was he kicked?' I asked, making as if to go.

'Nay, he was knocked over and collided with the feed

bin, I think. He's not badly hurt, Annie. It's his pride more'n anything.' He grinned.

I remembered that grin from my girlhood. He was always a cheerful lad, was David Annersley. I'd never known him all that well and he'd gone into the Army as soon as he was old enough during the war. When it was over, he decided to stay in as a career. He'd probably never have reappeared in Beckindale but for a rather serious chest injury which made him unfit for service.

As far as I'd gathered from my Dad's remarks, David was just giving a hand around the Verney's estate. David's father was employed by Mr Verney as a tractor driver and mechanic, and had a tied cottage on the land.

'Will you come in and have a cup of tea?' I invited.

'Glad to. I'm trying to catch up on my old acquaintances now I'm home for good,' he said.

I quickly took the wash-basket into the scullery and while I was there I tidied myself up a bit. Then I hurried back to make tea and set out home-made brandy snaps. At the sight of them, Dad said he thought he'd have a little tot of the real thing, to steady his nerves. We kept a little brandy 'for medicinal purposes', and I'll admit that the menfolk seldom invented reasons for getting access to it. I got it out and poured a measure for Dad, then felt it only polite to offer some to David.

'No thanks. I don't drink.'

'What, not at all?' Dad said, looking round at him in surprise.

'Nope. Saw too much of it in the Army. I got fed up of going out with t'lads, only to find their plan was just to get as tanked up as possible in as short a time as possible.'

'I bet they pulled your leg about being TT.'

David grinned. 'Oh, I can handle that. I'm a stubborn sort of feller. Well, are you all right now, Mr Pearson?'

'Aye, not too bad,' my father said, sipping his brandy.

'What did you do to the beast to make it knock you over?' I inquired, unwisely.

'No animal has ever knocked me over! Least, not on

purpose. It was a sheer accident. Mr Verney just didn't have control over the horse.'

'So it's Mr Verney's fault?'

'Nay, Annie, I never said that! I tell you, it were an accident.'

David nodded at me and finished off his cup of tea. 'I'd best get back,' he said. 'I borrowed the estate wagon – they'll be needing it, happen. Thanks for the tea.'

'Thank *you* for bringing Dad back'.

'A pleasure, I assure you.' He wandered to the door. 'I've often seen you from the slopes of Grey Top,' he remarked. 'When you look down from there you get a view of Emmerdale and the fields around it. I've seen you hurrying out to look into your baby's pram – when he cries, I suppose?'

'She,' I corrected. 'The baby's a little girl – Peggy.'

'Oh yes, that's right – Mr Pearson's mentioned his grand-daughter . . . You've got a little boy as well?'

'That's right. He starts school this year.'

'Goodness . . . Hardly seems possible. I remember you at school yourself.'

'You do? I was just thinking, when you drove up and spoke to me, that I remember you at school an' all.'

'Fancy that! Seems like yesterday, don't it?'

'Oh,' I said slowly, 'I don't know . . . A lot has happened.'

'I suppose so. But you still look almost exactly the same as you did when I left Beckindale.'

'Get away with you! You rushed off to join up the minute you were of age. I could only have been about fourteen then.'

'Well, you only look about fourteen still.'

'What, with my arms full of baby's washing?'

'Ahem,' Dad said in a loud voice. 'Well, thanks for giving me a hand, Dave. Tell Mr Verney I'm all right and I'll be back on the job as usual at six in the morning.'

'Righto,' David agreed, with his cheerful grin again. 'Nice to have caught up with you again, Annie. I'll drop by some time, if you've no objection.'

'None at all. You're always welcome, David.'

When he'd driven off, Dad said to me, 'There was no need to be all that welcoming to him, lass!'

'Why not? We owe him a bit of a thank-you for fetching you home.'

'Now o't'sort! Mr Verney asked him to.'

'Well, even so – he was looking after you, not just carting you about like a parcel.'

'Huh!' Dad said. 'He thought the whole thing was a great joke, if you want to know!'

'Oh, he's upset your dignity, is that it?'

'Is that all the sympathy I get?' he exclaimed. 'Kicked by a horse, and my own daughter –'

'I thought you said he didn't kick you?'

'Well, neither he did. It was just a way of speaking. If you're going to pick me up on every word I say –!'

'Now, Dad, don't be fractious,' I soothed. 'Come on, have another drop of brandy and then go upstairs for a lie-down.'

I could see he was divided between wanting to be a bit of an invalid so he could take the brandy, and insisting that the horse hadn't actually kicked him so he wasn't really hurt. In fact, he was a bit shaken, I could see that. So I coaxed him to drink up and have a rest.

It was odd, but Dad was always edgy with David Annersley from that day onwards. I could never see what it was that bothered him so much. He never actually said in so many words that he disliked David or disapproved of him – it would have been hard to do so, for a nicer, more open-hearted lad it would have been difficult to find. Yet there was always something that seemed to bother Dad. It is strange, isn't it, how people take up attitudes to others? I sometimes believe it's true, what 'psychic' experts say, that everybody has an aura and that some auras are sympathetic to each other. Nay, now – that's nonsense! But it's certainly true that my father never seemed quite easy when David Annersley was in the house. And not long since, when David came back to Beckindale on holiday, Dad took on as

7

if the man was Don Juan — and him a semi-invalid widower with a teenage daughter!

It might have been easier for Dad if Emily Tewkesbury hadn't taken up residence in Beckindale around Easter. She hadn't won the prize with her rural paintings the year before, but she was back with renewed plans to do a series, showing people at work. I seem to recall she'd got some sort of grant or allowance from a museum to paint 'country crafts'. Any road, she had money to pay for digs, and she got a room with the Annersleys in their cottage on the Verney estate, with the permission of Mr Verney.

Mr Verney was quite interested in Emily. I don't think he knew any more about painting than the rest of us, but he had some family portraits and landscapes hanging in the Hall, so I suppose that gave him a bit of a basis for talking about art to her.

From time to time I'd pass Emily with her easel set up — in Beckindale, happen, or on a hillside by a beck — and sometimes Mr Verney would be lounging beside her, flicking his leggings with a stick and offering criticism of her work.

'Seems to me the men of this district have nowt to do,' my father said sourly. '*I* don't have the time to walk a mile up-dale to see what a slip of a girl is painting!'

'Now, Dad. It's nice for her to have someone to talk to now and again. It must be a bit lonesome, sitting out there with her paints and her canvas.'

'She chose to do it, didn't she? If you want to know what I think, I think she'd rather be left alone to get on with it!'

'Oh, Emily likes a bit of a chat,' Jacob said.

'Oh aye? Did she tell you so?'

'You can see she likes it,' Jacob protested. 'She always looks up with a smile when you come along.'

'She does, does she! And which does she smile at more — you or George Verney?'

'Now, Dad!'

'I'm entitled to ask the question, Annie! At least George Verney is a single man!'

My husband stared at my father. 'I don't know what you're on about! Can't a chap say a civil word to a young lady wi'out having daft questions asked?'

All the same, my father wasn't the only person who was asking questions like that. When I look back now, I realise the whole of Beckindale was interested in what they saw as a rivalry of a sort, between my husband and George Verney, for the friendship of young Emily. Most of the people in the district wanted Mr Verney to get wed and settle down. Not that he was in any way unsettled. He lived mostly at the Hall, he looked after his lands, he took an interest in all the local activities. But he was, I imagine, about thirty. They thought it was time he chose a wife and started a family. You see, if the owner of a big estate has no children, there's no one to hand it to, and it was very much to the interest of Beckindale to have continuity at the Hall – to have an heir to take over the responsibilities, to play the same part in our lives as his father and grandfather had done.

So, on the whole, Beckindale wanted Mr Verney to get friendly with Emily, and they wanted Emily to like Mr Verney, and they more or less imagined a lovely wedding in the parish church and a big reception at the Hall afterwards.

Strange to say, Emily didn't seem to take to Mr Verney all that much.

'He's nice enough,' she murmured to me one day when I'd taken out a flask of tea to her as she sketched by the old mill. 'But . . . he's a bit stuffy.'

'Stuffy?'

'Conventional.'

'Well, you'd expect him to be conventional. He was brought up that way – public school, university, the war . . . He always knew he'd have to take over from his father one day. He was more or less trained for that.'

'That's what I mean! He hasn't a hint of originality in him!'

I laughed. 'Is that what you like? Originality?'

'Well, it makes people interesting! One of the things I like about your family, Annie, is that folk are a bit unex-

[99]

pected. Your father comes out with some surprising things now and again – about life in the old days, or his experiences in the First World War. And Jacob . . .'

'What about Jacob?'

'Jacob's extraordinary, you know. There's something . . . restless . . . unsatisfied . . . I don't know how to express it. He's like a falcon that's been tamed.'

'Tamed?' For some reason that I couldn't identify, that word hurt me. 'How do you mean, tamed?'

'Sometimes it seems to me he wasn't meant to be a farmer. You know, Annie, there's a rhythm in everybody – a sort of metronome beat that makes the pace of life – and Jacob's rhythm doesn't fit with the slow cycle of events on a farm. At least, that's how it seems to me.'

I shook my head. 'He's a farmer. He came back after the war to be a farmer. It's his own choice.'

She made no reply, but instead nibbled a biscuit and with her other hand made little additions to her charcoal sketch.

'Emily,' I said, 'I hope you don't tell Jacob he's not got the right rhythm for farming! He's fed up of it as it is – lack of money is a terrible handicap to him.'

I said all this in a half-teasing tone, but I meant it seriously. In a way, I understood what she meant about Jacob. But it was too late now to be changing his mind; Jacob was a farmer, it was the only thing he had any training for, and he couldn't swop horses in midstream now. I didn't want anybody encouraging him to think he was a misfit.

'It's a big pity he and George can't change places. If Jacob had the money to put into farming that George has, he'd do all sorts of new things –'

'Listen, love, new things aren't necessarily a good idea. The land is old – a lot older than we are. We shouldn't be rushing about on it, changing everything.'

'Oh, Annie! Don't be such a stick in the mud!'

'I'm not. It's just an instinct I have that we can do damage to our world if we throw away all the old things and rush after the new.' I hesitated. 'Have you heard what's happened on Luter Farm over in Melmshurt, where they've been using this new DDT?'

'DDT? That's the insecticide they discovered during the war, isn't it? I'd have thought *that* was a good thing.'

'Nay, Emily. On Luter Farm they raise some of the hounds for the Beckindale Hunt, and do you know what's happened? Some of the hound pups somehow licked up the DDT that was spread on something else, and it killed them.'

'Killed a puppy? But it's an insecticide —'

'It's a poison. If it can kill an insect it can kill a pup. What I'm trying to say, Emily, is that everything that's new isn't necessarily an improvement. And some of this big machinery they're putting in on the farms now — it's so heavy, lass, it weighs down on the soil and cakes it like rock.'

'You're not saying we should stick to old shire horses?' she teased. 'Those days are gone for ever.'

'I suppose so. All I'm saying is that it took the farming community thousands of years to reach the stage they were at when my Dad first started work. But since then, in about thirty years, everything is being altered. I wonder if it's a good thing to do away with two or three thousand years' worth of experience in the lifetime of one generation?'

'There you are!' she exclaimed. 'You're a lot more fun than George Verney, you Emmerdale folk! I never have a conversation with him that's anything like this!'

'And I've wasted enough time on this one,' I rejoined, 'I'd best get back and get the tea started.'

When I was indoors again and putting the chicken pie in the oven, I thought about what Emily had said. What a disappointment it would be to the rest of the world if they knew she found George Verney dull!

It didn't occur to me to worry that she thought my husband interesting.

CHAPTER EIGHT

THE BIGGEST ITEM in my diary for some months occurred when school resumed that year. Our Jack went into the infants' class.

That first day, I was lost and desolate. I took him to the door of the school where he was detached from my hand by Miss Nolton. He went in with her, his head turned towards me and his eyes full of tears that threatened to spill over his dark lashes on to his cheeks,

When it was time to fetch him back at dinnertime, I was at the school gate in good order. I was ready to comfort him and make it up to him that he'd been parted from me all morning.

Do you know what he said? 'Oh, hello, Ma. Are you coming to meet me every day? 'Cos I know my way home, you know.'

The little rascal. After I'd spent three hours breaking my

heart over him.

He took to school like a duck to water. Our Jack was a very clever child, although as he grew older he grew lazier He could learn anything he wanted to, but that word 'wanted' was the problem. Once the novelty of school wore off, he stopped bothering too much. But that was still in the future. For the first year of two he was full of enthusiasm, rushing home with paintings of models made in plasticine, and instructing me with great earnestness in how to make the letter 'A' with a pencil on a piece of paper.

I have to admit that, with Jack off my hands, life was a bit easier at home. Peggy was still too small to be up to mischief so I was able to catch up with quite a few household tasks I'd put off.

Emily was very interested in seeing the household tools of bygone days. I knew there were old-fashioned preserving pans in the attic, and some of the old tools that used to go with the inglenook fire before it was filled in with a kitchen range. She and I got there one day and came down with the trivet, the gridiron, and the chimney-crane.

We still say, on a hot day, 'It's like a gridiron.' Have you ever seen one? It was a thing rather like the wire tray in a modern grillpan, only made of iron and with a long handle – the handle was so that the cook could stand a long way from the fierce heat of the fire and the spitting fat from the meat. The gridiron was used for broiling steaks and chops over an open fire. It must have been one of the messiest cooking implements ever invented, because there was no way of collecting the grease, which must have dripped straight into the fire, I suppose.

The chimney-crane was an absolutely marvellous thing. An upright iron bar was set into a square stone block to give it stability. On this, a horizontal arm was forged. There was a collection of hooks on the bar, from which the various pots could be slung over the heat. Attached to the upright there was a sort of C-shaped curve with studs on it and a lever which could be raised or lowered by means of these studs, so you could have the pot higher or lower over the flame. It was a beautiful piece of blacksmithing. We showed it to Frank Blakey later, and he said he hoped no one would ever ask him to make one because he thought it was beyond him. Yet in the days when it was made, every village blacksmith must have been turning them out.

Downstairs in my kitchen I had the old butter-churn and the butter moulds, still in use; from time to time I'd make a little fresh buter for our own use, or for a Women's Institute show. Patterns of our wooden moulds included a primrose, a robin, and the initials J.S. which must have been the initials of the farm-wife who had it made – probably Jane Sugden, the wife of the first Sugden we have a record of as tenant of Emmerdale Farm over a hundred years ago.

Up in the attic we found the cheese-press that matched the butter churn, clearly made by the same joiner; beautifully smoothed oaken staves so finely fitted together that they scarcely needed the copper band around the outside. The cheese-press hadn't been in use for a long time.

For about four weeks, Gran and I tried out various different cheese recipes with the cheese-press. I'd never have had the time if our Jack had been underfoot. But I should have known it wouldn't last, because of course, having newly started at school, he caught every cold and every sniffle that was going. Every mother will know what I mean. The moment school reopens, all the children pass all their germs to one another. I suppose it's all part of the process of building up immunities, so that by the time they leave school the youngsters are able to withstand most of the common germs. But it certainly is tiresome for mothers, as children come home first with a cold, then with a cough, then with spots that turn out to be chicken pox, then with a sniffle that turns out to be measles, and so on and so on.

I remember I was sitting with Jack reading him a story, while he snuggled in bed with a cold, and I heard Dad come in and switch on the radio in the kitchen. By and by he came up to inquire how the invalid was doing, and murmured: 'Know what the chap on the six o'clock news was saying?

There's been a notification of foot-and-mouth disease in Hampshire.'

'Oh dear,' I said, rather absent-minded. 'Poor souls. I hope it won't be bad.'

When I think of it now –! I simply didn't take it in. I'd no idea how bad it was going to be, nor how many of us were going to shudder with dread at the news bulletins from then on.

Foot-and-mouth disease was given that name because the animals get little ulcers in the mouth and between the toes or where the toes would be if it's a hoofed animal. It's caused by a virus, and in recent times a lot more has been discovered about it. But twenty-five years ago knowledge was still not as profound as it might have been; there was certainly no injection that could be given against it.

Part of farming legend in my young days was the outbreak in Scotland in the Twenties. It used to be said – I don't know with how much truth – that every cow in Lowland Scotland was slaughtered at that time.

Every farmer is terrified of foot-and-mouth disease among his stock. The only treatment is complete isolation of the farm and the slaughter of all the animals within its boundaries.

You may say it's cruel and unnecessary. Healthy animals are killed along with infected beasts. It seems unjust. All I can tell you is that the disease *must* be stopped. It's true, livestock can recover from foot-and-mouth, but condition deteriorates, milk yields swoop downwards and calves are usually stillborn. What you are left with is a sick herd which may take ten years to recover. Moreover, you're never sure it's free from infection. That herd – every beast in it – is a danger to every healthy animal within miles.

It's still a bit of a mystery how foot-and-mouth disease is spread. Some say that migrating birds bring the virus with them from countries further to the south, where it's much more common than in Britain. At the time of speaking, foot-and-mouth was almost endemic in France – I mean, it occured there regularly. Things have been cleaned up since then. But in those days a lot of farmers thought that birds coming to Britain from France and Italy for the summer might bring the virus with them.

I believe I'm right in saying, however, that the source of the outbreak that cost Emmerdale its livestock was traced to bone meal imported from South America. Bone meal, as its name implies, is made from bones – bones left over after the meat has been stripped off for sale. South America – particularly Argentina – exported huge amounts of beef to Britain, both carcass meat and as corned beef and so on. Bones from beef cattle were ground down for sale as fertilizer and animal feed. But, if the product wasn't treated with enough hygienic care, the virus of foot-and-mouth disease could still survive in the bone meal. And, in South America, foot-and-mouth disease was commonplace.

Imports from South America were suspended for a time, I recall. But by then it was too late. The epidemic had taken off in Britain. It began in South England, in Hampshire, in October. There were a couple of other notifications. In November a bigger outbreak was reported in a farm near Eastbourne. Swine fever, which is the name given to the same disease among pigs, also began to be heard of.

Slowly, slowly, it travelled north from its first appearance. It began to come home to farmers throughout the country that the outbreaks weren't being contained. I can't describe to you the horror of listening to reports on the radio and realising that each one was bringing that terrible tide closer to our own harbour.

In January of the following year, after a very worrying winter during which both my husband and my father kept checking their livestock, we heard with sinking hearts that an outbreak had been notified in Durham.

'It won't come here,' Jacob kept saying. 'We're so much higher up than most other farmers . . .'

But even if it didn't actually come to our farm, the effects were very bad. Markets were cancelled, the transporting of livestock in a notified area was absolutely forbidden. So you couldn't sell or buy a beast.

Breakfast at our house was a long-term undertaking. Jacob always had a cup of tea before he went out at five-thirty to milk, and my father would share that and lend a hand. But he always liked to be at Verney's by six-thirty at the latest, so I used to have his breakfast ready for him although Jacob would still be finishing off and cleaning down. Usually by that time the children would be awake; Peggy was no problem, she could be settled down again until it was time to bath her, but our Jack liked to be up and about to see what was happening so I'd give him a piece of toast or an apple to be going on with while I dealt with the menfolk.

Then Jacob and Gippo would come in. Gippo was supposed to have his meals with his mother at their van, but I never protested when he took to coming in for breakfast. With all respect to Gran, I think my breakfast was better than hers – she provided grilled bacon or sausage but for some reason I never understood, she didn't make toast and the only cereal she'd allow was porridge cooked overnight in a haybox.

One morning Jacob and Gippo didn't appear. I had the bacon and mushrooms in the oven keeping hot, but the time kept going by and the mushrooms weren't improving. They're funny things, mushrooms; they seem to lose heat quicker than anything else that gets cooked, and I've often thought that the plate on which I serve them is hotter than the mushrooms.

At length I put a cardigan over my head against the rain and ran out to call them. I found them standing by the door of the mistle, silent, looking in at the cows. They'd milked but they hadn't turned the last set out to the pasture.

'Come on,' I urged. 'Your bacon's getting frizzled.'

They turned towards me. One look at my husband's white face told me everything.

'Oh, no!' I gasped.

'Looks like it, lass.'

Gippo shook his head with weary acceptance. 'They've got it in Fellendale.'

'I suppose it had to come to Beckindale.'

'But I thought . . . I hoped . . .'

'So did I, Annie.'

'You're sure it's foot-and-mouth?'

'Nay, I'm not sure. But if it's not that, I don't know what else it is.'

'What are you going to do?'

'I'll go and fetch the vet.'

'Come and have your breakfast first.'

Gippo came with a certain amount of eagerness. Jacob followed more slowly, and scarcely ate a morsel. As soon as he'd finished he got into our truck and set off for Hotten to see Mr Riceyman.

Meanwhile I sent Gippo with a message to my father at Verney's. One of the important things about foot and mouth disease is to limit the extent of the outbreak as far as possible. I'd no idea whether there had been any signs of it at Verney's but my father needed to know what had happened at Emmerdale; he had to take what precautions he could for the stock in his care.

It's a common fallacy that only cattle get foot and mouth. Other animals get the disease, sometimes in a different form. Even humans aren't immune; one of my friends, Lucy Jarrett, was terrible ill for months with foot-and-mouth disease. It sounds like a joke, doesn't it? But I assure you it's nothing to laugh at.

For all these reasons, my father needed to be given immediate information about the suspected sickness in our mistle. Gippo came back about an hour and a half later with a note for me from Dad.

'Dear Annie, I'm thinking over what to do. Mr Verney's at Leeds until about tea-time, and I'll ask him what he thinks is best. But I've a feeling it would be a good thing if I stayed here at Verney's until things clear up. It wouldn't be fair to anyone for me to be going back and forth between Emmerdale and here and, any road, I'd be honour bound to stay away from work if there really is an outbreak at Emmerdale. I'll send word later.'

I wasn't surprised by his attitude. He was very taken up with the stock at Verney's, so the last thing he'd want to do would be to carry any germs to them. Moreover, while the danger lasted he'd want to be on the spot at Verney's so as to help in any way he could.

Jacob came back with Mr Riceyman – he'd had to wait while the vet dealt with other clients. The two of them went out to the mistle and then I saw them going out to the pasture. It seemed a century until they reappeared.

I watched them plodding over the rain-soaked meadow and then across the track to our yard and inside our gate. I could see from the way Jacob's shoulders were slumped that the news was bad.

I had coffee ready for them. Mr Riceyman sank down with a sigh. He looked nearly as upset as Jacob. Mind you, it was no wonder – he'd been out and about all over the district for weeks now, dealing with alarms over the disease at first but now of course beginning to verify its existence.

'What's the verdict?' I said, though I hardly needed to have it put into words.

'It seems fairly certain. All the symptoms are there. I'll put up a warning for the moment and by tomorrow or the next day we'll know for certain.'

'Are you going to inform the Ministry?'

'Yes, I'll ring when I get back and say there's another suspected case.' He took his cup of coffee and dunked his ginger biscuit in it. 'Have you got supplies of disinfectant?'

'Some, but not enough.'

'You'd better come back with me, Sugden, and collect more.'

'Righto.'

Just at that moment Emily drove up in her little tin Lizzie.

'Lord above, what's that?' Mr Riceyman exclaimed.

'She's an artist. Doing paintings and sketches of old farm crafts and implements.'

'You'd better warn her off. Trouble enough without young lasses trekking infection from one place to another.'

Emily came in, shaking rain off her jacket. 'Hello, you look glum,' she said, much too brightly.

'No wonder. Seems we've got foot-and-mouth at Emmerdale.'

'Oh.' The smile was wiped off her face. She sat down next to Jacob. 'I'm so sorry,' she murmured.

'Aye,' he sighed, and nodded at her as if her sympathy made all the difference.

'Is that right, you're going round painting things on the farms?' the vet demanded.

'Well . . . yes . . . why do you ask?'

'Look here, young lady, this is the very worst time to be travelling from place to place. If you take my advice, you'll pack it in for the time being.

'But . . . I can't, very well. I'm staying at a cottage on Mr Verney's estate.'

'Mr Verney won't thank you if you walk the disease into his barns on your wellingtons.'

'No, I suppose he won't . . .'

The talk went round and round while Mr Riceyman drank two cups of coffee, and polished off almost my whole baking of ginger biscuits. Then he said: 'It'd make more sense if you stayed here at Emmerdale for the time being, Miss Tewkesbury. No sense in going back on Verney's land if you don't have to. So far, he's got no trace of the disease among his livestock.'

'Oh, I couldn't intrude—'

'This is no time for polite misgivings, lass. Annie, can you put her up?'

'Well, I—'

'I could stay with Grannie Lee, perhaps—'

'You wouldn't like that,' Jacob put in. 'It's a bit cramped, unless you're reared to it. Nay, you'd be better off here. We can giver her a bed, can't we Annie?'

'If Dad decides to stay at Verney's while the emergencey is on, she could have Dad's room.'

In the end that was the way things turned out. Dad changed places with Emily – he got her room at the Annersleys' cottage and she got his room at Emmerdale. I did suggest at one point that it might perhaps make more sense if Emily went home to her parents for a bit, but she had a lot of work to do on her series of paintings of country life if she were to get it ready in time. 'I've got to hand it into the selection committee at Harrogate,' she explained, 'and then, win or lose, I've got the chance of a one-man show in London in the autumn. I'll lose al that if I don't get on with my work.'

We were all taking it for granted that the outbreak of foot-and-mouth at Emmerdale would be confirmed. And we were right.

I'm not going to go on about what happened next because it's too harrowing. I've sometimes heard townsfok say that farmers are very unemotional about their beasts, that they treat producing meat and milk like a factory process. Well, all I can say is, they ought to take a look at a farmer's face when his herd is destroyed. It is the most heartbreaking think in the world. You know, every milking cow has a name – not just a pedigree-book name (if you've got a pedigree herd) but a name that the milking staff call her by. Does anyody really think you can see Buttercup and Rosie and Tottie-True and Jemima standing in the meadows with their heads hanging down and their legs going weak, without feeling utterly stricken? Does anybody believe you can say goodbye to those beasts without tears pricking at the back of your eyes?

I've always believed that those weeks scarred our Jack. I think it was at that time that he subconsciously made up his mind not to follow his father into farming. Jack was very fond of the animals, you know – not in a sentimental way, but he seemed to have a way of identifying with them. It was impossible to keep from him what was happening – if we'd tried not to say anything, he'd have heard it from the other children at school. And in any case the stench of the burning was everywhere, even though the fields where the Ministry man was disposing of the carcasses was a long way off, on the far side of our land.

It wasn't a good time for any of us – except for our Peggy, happen. She was too little to know what was going on, and she saw a lot of folk hanging around the farmhouse and quite enjoyed it. And for me, perhaps it was less hurtful than for the men, for I could get on with household chores I'd put by because I was too busy.

A couple of years before, I'd bought paint and wallpaper for the upstairs rooms, which had never been redecorated since I moved into Emmerdale after my marriage. I got going on that. Emily elected to help me. It was funny how bad she was at it, considering she was an artist! She was all right at handling a paintbrush, but she'd no idea about measuring and cutting paper.

I don't know why she felt she had to take a hand in the redecorating. I suppose she felt that, since she'd been more or less wished on us for the duration, she ought to get totally invovled, she ought to 'suffer' with us. By and by, though, she realised there were marvellous views of the country from our upstairs windows. Even in the rain – or happen, particularly in the rain, when she could see the moisture glistening on the canopy of the trees and the way the clouds hung over the valleys – the view was beautiful. So when she began to drift away and do sketches, and then later asked if I would mind if she set up her easel in one of the bedrooms that we weren't redecorating, I encouraged her. And then the rain stopped, and she went outdoors to get on with this important series of country life paintings that had to be finished.

Jacob meanwhile had a lot to do at first. He closed all the gates and openings on to our land except for the chief entries, where he put baths or tubs of disinfectant so that visitors could rinse their boots. It was important not to walk the virus of foot-and-mouth from our farm to anyone else's. To head off walkers and picknickers, who had a right to use footpaths, he put up big notices: 'Foot-and-mouth – Please do not cross this land.' It had its effect. We didn't see a single rambler all through the time we stayed in quarantine. It made a difference to us, oddly enough. We'd grumble from time to time about walkers leaving gates open and picnickers spreading litter, but we quite liked seeing them about at the weekends. When they didn't appear, we felt even more isolated.

Once al the initial jobs had been done, Jacob was at liberty to go about the farm schedule. There was hay to get in. Jacob and Gippo did this without help – it was better that way and because they weren't going to help anyone else and there was therefore no rush, they took their time about it and did it well. In those days there was still controversy about whether foot and mouth virus could be carried on grass stems, so the hay Jacob cut couldn't be taken to any other farm. But that didn't matter – we generally kept our hay for our own use, having almost no surplus for sale. When they'd finished with the hay-maker they washed it down well at the exit to our land and left it to be taken on to the next farmer who needed it.

After that there were jobs to be done. The weather had turned very fine indeed – in fact, it was almost too dry, and if we'd had stock to care for we'd have been a bit overworked making sure they had enough water on some of the upper pastures.

Taking of the upper pastures reminds me of the sheep. Sheep aren't affected by foot-and-mouth disease in the same way as cattle, although they have their own diseases. Our lambing was over by the time we found the sickness in our milk herd, so the flock was up on the higher slopes and safely away from infections that seem to follow foot-and-mouth. However, there was little chance of bringing any of them down and taking them to market; severe restrictions were in action on the movement of animals, including healthy animals, because movement of any kind seemed to spread the disease.

But any road, Jacob wasn't interested in sheep. He left them to themselves once lambing was over, although Gippo liked to go on the uplands just to cast an eye over them. Upland sheep are very hardy, you see. They can live through almost every kind of weather except snow which

8

covers the grass too deep, or extreme drought.

Jacob tidied up the yard and mended implements and repaired field-walls. For a time he was very hard at work. Then the pointlessness of it seemed to hit him. He lost heart, and I'd see him from my kitchen window, wandering about with his hands in his trouser pockets.

He'd go and watch Emily at her painting. It became so much a matter of course that when he didn't come in for elevenses, and I took out coffee in a flask to Emily, I'd take some for him too.

'You Gorgios are a rum lot,' Grannie Lee said to me as I came home from his chore one morning. 'If a Romany found her husband hanging around another woman, she'd scratcg his eyes out, not take him coffee and cake!'

'Get on with you, Gran. It's as well he has someone to talk to. It helps him get rid of his restlessness.'

'Oh, does it? It stops him getting on with renewing the doors on the machinery store, though.'

'He's not fond of carpentry, Gran.'

'He's not fond of most things, if you ask me! He's right narked because Verney's land has escaped untouched in the foot-and-mouth epidemic.'

'That not true. Like every other farmer, he's pleased when a neighbour gets off unscathed in this business.'

'Not from the way I've heard him talk! He's annoyed that you dad don't come home either – seems to think he's kicking his heels at Verney's.'

'What's the matter? Why are you being so sharp about him?'

She snipped busily at the paper flowers she was making. 'He makes me angry.' she admitted. 'He's got so much that other men would envy. Why can't he be grateful for what he's got, instead of day-dreaming about a prize herd and an extended farm with a lass that doesn't know fact from fancy? I'll tell you this, Annie – he wouldn't waste his time talking like that to you. He knows you'd pull him up and point out it was all castles in the air.'

I studied her. 'This quarantine's getting you down too,

Gran, isn't it?'

She sighed and shrugged. 'Us Romanies don't like being boxed in, I suppose.'

'But you've been here on this site for a long time now, by your own choice. You like it, don't you?'

'Oh aye. Never been happier. But it's having the feeling that we're expected to stay tied up here – that we're locked in.'

'You're not locked in, love. If you take all the proper precautions, you can leave.'

'And just think how everybody would glare at us if we did. "Spreading foot and mouth – typical of a gipsy, they don't care what they do." Nay, nay, we'll bide where we are for now. But, Annie . . . when the epidemic dies down, happen Gippo and me'll take a little turn round the country, just to stretch our legs. We've been in one place for along time now.'

'Oh,' My heart sank at the news. I'd grown so accustomed to having Gran around that I couldn't think how we'd get on without her. 'You'd come back?'

'Aye, lass, you can bet on that! We've got friends here, my son and me.

Harvest came on, and the men got the barley in. Our crop was rather thin that year – the weather had been so surprisingly dry that it didn't hearten up. Seeding Cut that year was a much-diminished affair, held on the land of Lucy Matherson, a woman farmer who had never gone in for livestock and whose farm therefore was entirely free from any danger. I don't think she was very pleased about it; she was a funny old girl, a spinster in the sense we used to use that word – totally uninterested in men, inclined to look down on married women, and suspicious of children. She couldn't say no to having Last Cut on her wheat-field but I think she felt the whole thing was scandalous! And so it is, I suppose, if you go back to its pagan origins.

There had been no reports of foot-and-mouth in the country for quite a time now. The official from the Min. of Ag. and Fish. did a tour and called all the local vets in a conference. Restrictions were lifted; the area was declared safe. We were free to move about without let or hindrance.

We all had our own small celebrations. Mine was to take the children on the bus to Hotten and buy them icecream. I still remember our Peggy in her puch-chair, icecream running down her little round chin and a blissful expression on her face.

Jacob was thinking about how to spend the compensation he'd get for having had his cows destroyed. The government insisted on this method of containing foot-and-mouth so there was a government scheme for compensation, but you know how it is – it's never as much as you've lost. Jacob had some insurance against various troubles that beset a farmer, but once again, not enough.

From time to time he'd get the farm record books out and do sums about how to deal with the problem of replacing the milk herd. My father, who of course had come home again now that the scare was over, offered suggestions now and again. But Jacob would shake his head and go off into a long reverie. He couldn't seem to make up his mind.

Now that there was no reasons why he shouldn't walk about freely, without having to wash his boots on going out and coming in, he took to going down to the Woodpack of an evening. Dad didn't go with him. 'Home's good enough for me,' he said. 'Eeh, I missed thee, lass! Mrs Annersley's a good soul, but she's not a patch on thee as a cook!'

Emily had gone back to her digs in the Annersleys' cottage. To my great regret, Grannie Lee and Gippo had pulled up stumps and driven away for a little road-travelling. 'You don't need us just at t'moment,' she pointed out. 'Harvest's over, nowt much to do until you man makes up his mind whether to replace the milk herd. Let's us go about for a fortnight or so, love. We'll be back.'

I felt strangely forlorn just around that time. Everything seemed to be changing, and I didn't quite know whether it was for the better or the worse.

One day I was in Beckindale for some groceries. Mrs Annersley was just about to go into the village shop as I came out. She paused to chat with me.

We talked about the aftermath of the foot-and-mouth, which tended still to be the chief topic of conversation. Mrs Annersley hadn't really had any problems on that score because her husband's employer had had no infection among his stock. I think she felt a bit guilty that she hadn't had as bad a time as some of us.

'You know,' she said, 'if ever you feel that *'you'd* like an evening at t'Woolpack, I'd be glad to babysit for you.'

I was a bit puzzled by the way she said *'you'* with so much emphasis. 'It's very kind of you,' I replied. 'My father would babysit, I suppose, if I wanted to go. But somehow . . .'

'He does ask you to go, that husband of yours?' she insisted. She was a straightforward soul, Mrs Annersley – no beating about the bush with her.

'Oh, I could have an evening out any time . . .'

'Then why don't you?'

'I . . . er . . .' The fact was, Jacob didn't seem to put the idea forward.

'When was the last time you and he had a night out?'

'Well, we had a day in Harrogate last year.'

'Last year! It's ridiculous! Men are hopeless! Sitting chatting in the Woolpack with Emily, and never thinking to take you there or to a picture-house or something!'

I think she must have seen my face change at what she said about Emily. She closed her lips and looked at me with her frank blue eyes. 'You didn't know he meets Emily there?'

'Oh, it's natural – they're good friends.'

She shifted from foot to foot. 'She's a nice lass,' she agreed. 'I wouldn't have her in my house if I didn't think a lot of her. But I wonder if she realises what she's doing?'

'She's not doing anything–'

'I'm not so sure. Would you like me to speak to her about it?'

I suppose everybody has a tether that they come to the end of. That was when I came to the end of mine.

'Nay, Mrs Annersley,' I said. 'I'll see to it myself.'

CHAPTER NINE

THERE ARE SOME folk who rather enjoy a row, I think. If they're not in the middle of an emotional drama, they feel something's missing. I'm not a bit like that. I hate raised voices and name-calling.

But when the time comes for straight speaking, I daresay I'm as able as anyone else to have my say. All the same, I don't believe I ever rush in and say the first thing that comes into my mind.

On my way to find Emily, I thought about what I was going to tell her. I knew where to find her, for I'd passed her on my way to Beckindale: she was painting on the southern bank of the river. I'd got the push-chair with me, and a load of shopping – it wasn't exactly the best equipment for going into battle. But now that the moment had come to speak, I felt there was no use shirking it. So I took the footpath along the river bank, much to the entertainment of our Peggy, who'd thought we were going home to dinner.

Emily heard me coming. She paused in her work and turned to look over her shoulder.

'Good gracious, Annie!' she exclaimed, seeing me shoving the pushchair along the uneven path. 'Is anything wrong?'

'That remains to be seen,' I said. I parked the push-chair, paused a moment to give Peggy half a biscuit to keep her happy then came to Emily's side. 'I want to talk to you about Jacob,' I said.

She met my gaze with her open, bright smile. 'What about Jacob?' she asked.

'He spends a lot of time with you.'

'Yes, I suppose he does. I think it helps him to talk things over with me.'

'Do you really think it does?'

She frowned. 'What?'

'Do you really think you're a help to Jacob?'

'Well, I . . . It must be a help to have someone to try out your ideas on.'

'What do you say to him, when he talks about his plans?'

'What do I say to him? What a funny question. What do you mean, Annie?' She was looking very perplexed, a little distressed. 'There's nothing wrong in it, if that's what's worrying you. He talks, I listen – it's almost all about the farm and what he thinks of doing with it.'

'I never said different, lass. I'm not accusing you of owt wrong in the ordinary sense. But do you really think you help my man by encouraging him to build castles in the air all the time?'

'Jacob's got plans, Annie. He wants to improve the farm. When he buys new stock, he wants to improve the breed –'

'Oh aye? Has he discussed how he'll pay for the service of the bull? Has he put our name down for one of Mr Verney's prize animals? The fees are pretty high, you know.'

'Fees?' she echoed, looking baffled.

'You didn't know you have to pay for the services of a

pedigree bull? It doesn't come free, you know. And there's a waiting list.'

'Annie!'

'Do you think I'm being coarse, putting those points in front of you? It's for a reason, lass. Farming isn't a business you can dream about too much. It's concerned with realities. If Jacob's been talking about the realities with you, then I've nowt to disapprove of. But if he hasn't talked facts and figures – if you've let him run on telling you he's going to do this and that wi'out thought of the costs involved, then I'm claiming that you're not helping him.'

'But Annie – everyone's entitled to a dream! What would life be like if we didn't have our hopes and plans?'

I sighed. 'You have hopes of winning a prize wi' these paintings – yes?'

'You know I have.'

'So you sit here, working away on your canvas, getting cramp in your shoulder I daresay . . . You know full well you won't win a prize unless the paintings are finished in time to go before the selection committee.'

'Of course.'

'Jacob's got hopes and plans. He wants to improve the farm. One of his schemes involves starting again with better cows, but that means fewer animals for the money he'll get as compensation. If we have fewer cows, we get less milk. That means less money coming in. The only way to earn the money for putting the cows in calf to a bull that will improve the herd is to produce something else meanwhile – we've either got to grow something to sell, or hire out to someone else for part of the time, or sell such equipment as we've got. Tell me what figures Jacob's discussed with you, then I'll tell you how much help you've been to him.'

While I'd been speaking, Emily had been slowly colouring up. 'He's never talked to me in those terms,' she said in a low voice.

'I never thought he had, Emily. The minute it comes down to brass tacks, it stops being a dream, doesn't it? And dreams are what my man's living on at the present.'

'But dreaming . . . planning . . . is a stage in reaching reality, Annie. I've no doubt Jacob has all those facts and figures worked out – he just doesn't mention them to me –'

'Nay, lass, he hasn't. He does almost no paperwork these days. There's a pile of stuff in t'dresser drawer that he ought to deal with, but he doesn't.'

'He'll get round to it, Annie! You don't understand – after what he's been through, he needs time to recover.'

'But the land won't wait, Emily!' I gestured with my hand towards the slope of the dale, where the autumn colours were coming into the bracken. 'You know what it says in the Bible – 'As ye sow, so shall ye reap'. Decisions have got to be made soon. Dreams are no good to the land. You can't sow and reap dreams. The fields need seed, they need the plough and the drill on them. If we're to have cows in the mistle, we've got to go to market and buy them.'

Emily jumped up, making her easel sway with the vigour of her movement. 'It's all very well to accuse me! If you were more sympathetic to him, perhaps he'd talk to you about all this!'

'Sympathetic! Emily, he's my husband. If he'll come to me with any plan that he's thought through, I'll go along with him, whatever he wants to do. If he wants to give up farming and try his hand at summat else – summat he feels a call to – I'll pull up stumps and go wi' him. But I've got to be sympathetic to more than my man.' I nodded towards our Peggy, sitting sleepily in her push-chair watching the sunlight dancing on the river's surface. 'I've got a son and a daughter to feed and clothe. They deserve some sympathy too.'

'But don't you see, something's wrong if Jacob can't discuss things with you without being totally practical all the time –'

'Aye, lass, something's wrong. I know it. Mine isn't a perfect marriage and I'm not saying it is. And you're not helping.'

'That's not fair! People have a right to exchange ideas, to explore schemes and ideas. We don't always have to weigh everything up and ask 'Am I helping, am I hindering' – discussion is good in itself. That's what makes mankind different from the rest of the animal kingdom, Annie. We can talk to each other. Conversation has a value in itself.'

'Are you talking about 'art for art's sake'? I've heard that phrase. Talk for talk's sake – is that it? You can afford that, happen. Jacob can't. And I don't think many folk can. Seems to me I've read that in days gone by folk used to sit around and have conversations – and right good fun it must have been, too. But a farmer has to work first, talk after. You're letting Jacob do it t'other way round.'

'But Jacob has a right to friendships, like every other man! He has a right to use his own time as he wants to.'

'I'll tell you this, Emily. I'd rather my man talked and had friendships with other farmers.'

We stared at each other. After a moment she said: 'You're being very hard, Annie. I didn't think you could be hard.'

'I'm being driven to it.'

'I think you're wrong. If I were to pack and go, it wouldn't change Jacob.'

'Happen it wouldn't. We won't know, unless you do it.'

I saw her eyes fill with tears. 'You mean you want me to leave?'

'Oh, Emily . . .' I couldn't bring myself to say 'yes' to that.

'You've always made me so welcome. I thought you liked me.'

'I do, lass. I do.' I paused a long time before going on. 'But if it comes to a choice between thee and the welfare of my family, I have to choose my family.'

'I'm not a danger to your family, Annie. That's the last thing I want to be.'

I moved away to take hold of the push-chair. 'I've said my say, Emily.'

'You really want me to go?'

'That's up to you. I came here to let you know that I think you shouldn't let Jacob talk to you about his plans for Emmerdale wi'out nailing him down to the facts. If you think you can talk facts and figures wi' him, then I've no objections. But if it's to go on being castles-in-Spain, you're doing him no favour.' I began to push Peggy off along the path.

Emily called: 'Annie!'

'Yes?'

'It's about time for me to take my paintings to the selection committee anyhow.'

'You know best about that.'

'And I've got to follow up on that one-man show in London.'

'You see?' I said. 'You've got to get down to brass tacks, haven't you?'

'I suppose so,' she mumbled, and began to busy herself dismantling her easel.

When I got home it was a bit late to put the vegetables on for dinner so I whipped up a salad. Dad never liked salad with hot meat so I knew I'd have grumbles from him about it. But he was pressed for time so he ate up quickly and was on his way out again while Jacob and our Jack were still finishing their pudding.

'Willie Wyatt's dad is going to market tomorrow,' our Jack announced as he spooned custard from the edge of the dish into his mouth. He liked to give us information about the goings-on among his school friends. 'He's taking Willie with him. Can we go to market, dad?'

'Nay, there's nowt at Loudwick I want to see.'

'We haven't been to Loudwick for ages and ages,' Jack persisted. 'Willie's dad is going to buy him a budgie. Can we have a budgie?'

'A budgie?' Jacob exclaimed. 'That's daft, is that! There's plenty o' birds around Emmerdale without buying little things in cages.'

'Can we have another collie, then, Dad?'

We'd had to have Moss put down during the foot-and-mouth epidemic. He was a good old dog, was Moss. I didn't fancy the idea of a successor to him – but if we were going to go on raising sheep, we needed a dog. So I waited with interest to see what Jacob would say.

'I'm thinking on it,' he murmured.

Jack got up to get ready for the return trip to school. I had an arrangement with a neighbour to share the collecting and taking of our children, and it was Jack's turn to run down to the lane-end to meet Mrs Soames and her Dinah.

I cleaned up our Peggy and took her upstairs for her nap. As I came down, Jacob was opening the outside door to go out.

'Just a minute, lad,' I called. 'Can I have a word wi' thee?'

'What about, Annie? I want to go out and see if the water's coming up in the Stony Spring yet.'

'That can wait, Jacob. If the spring's going to start again, it'll start whether you're there to watch it or not.'

'What's up, then?' he asked, coming back indoors. It struck me how unwilling he was to stay and talk to me. My heart sank. We really had been drifting apart. Was it my fault?

'Jacob, I want to know what you plan to do about the farm,' I said, straight out.

'You know I'm still giving it some thought. It's not a thing I can settle in five minutes.'

'It's September, lad. Winter'll soon be upon us.'

'I know what time of year it is!'

'Nay, Jacob,' I said, hurt at his tone. 'Sit thee down, love. Let's have a talk about what you've got in mind.'

'I'm not in the mood to talk at the moment.'

'Shall us talk about it this evening, then? We need to get down to it some time or other. I need to know what sort of help you'll expect from me.'

He sat down slowly. 'Help from you?' he said. 'But you're so busy with the children and the house –'

'Oh, you know I've always been able to fit in other things. If it's going to be a matter of getting every penny together, I could do more with the poultry. There'll be the usual orders for Christmas geese, of course, and I can feed up some chickens too for sale – farm-bred chickens still fetch a good price. I was thinking, too, that the things Grannie Lee makes could find a market.'

'That Grannie Lee makes? Like what, for instance?'

'Paper flowers. They're right pretty.'

'Good heavens, Annie, no one round here wants paper flowers when t' hedges are full of real'uns.'

'Not here,' I insisted. 'Harrogate, happen. Or those holiday camps. Mrs Soames was telling me they have little shops that sell souvenirs in holiday camps.

One or two of our friends had had holidays in holiday camps. They were the 'in' thing just then. Seems incredible to me that I thought they were tremendously expensive – at about six pounds a week all in!

'All that's small beer, Annie. The main thing is what to do about the milk herd.'

'I agree. Have you made up your mind on that?'

'I just told you,' he said with irritation. 'It can't be settled in a rush.'

I hesitated. This was the sensitive area. 'What kind of thing will help you to make up your mind?' I ventured. 'Have you got all the information you need? The Ministry has statistics, I'm sure, if you were to write to them –'

'Ministries!' he burst out. 'What do *they* know? Their experts work in test stations with ideal conditions!'

'Well, there are lots of milk producers in the county who could give you some information about milk yields.' I didn't dare name Mr Verney. Mr Verney hadn't built up a prize herd without working out costs and outgoings. In fact, my father could have given Jacob a lot of inside information if only he'd been willing to listen to him. But for the moment, all I wanted was to plant the idea in his mind that time was going on, that a decision would have to be made soon, and that background information for that decision was available if he would only ask for it.

'I haven't time to go round the country asking for information,' he retorted.

'Seems to me, love – one thing you've got plenty of at the moment is time. Until you make up your mind and start again, you're just *marking* time, really.'

'Oh, if you're going to criticise me —'

'Nay, nay, I'm not criticising. I'm just saying — whenever you feel the moment's come to take the plunge, I'm with you. It'd be nice to have a bit of warning if I'm going to have to do anything special to play a part or earn extra cash. Just let me know, eh?'

'I wish you stop pushing me!' he burst out. 'I've told you I'm still thinking on. That should be enough.'

I'd been moving about clearing the table while I talked, because I didn't want to make him feel I was having a confrontation. But at those words I stopped and looked full at him.

I didn't say anything. I couldn't. I was hurt. I'm not one to wilt in the face of rough words but there was something so thoughtless in his tone that I found my voice had failed me.

He met my eyes and we stared at each other. I thought how haggard he looked. Why, he's making himself ill, I thought. He doesn't know what to do and the anxiety is making him ill.

'Jacob,' I said at length, 'I'm sorry if I seemed to be pushing you. I'm sorry, lad.'

He looked away. After a moment he got up and went to the door. 'I'll go and look at the spring,' he said.

'Aye.'

'It's important to know if our water supply is coming in again after this dry spell.'

'Aye.'

'There's such a load to think about!'

'It is a load, Jacob,' I agreed. 'But you needn't carry it alone, you know.'

After he'd gone I gave up siding the dishes and sat down by the table. I didn't know if I'd done any good by speaking to him. I was very worried. I'd more or less told Emily Tewkesbury she'd be best to clear out — but what would Jacob do without someone like that to talk to? Happen I'd done a very wrong thing.

When we'd had our teas that evening, I hoped he'd sit

down with my father and me to talk. It may well be that he would have done so, except that Dad was in one of his fractious moods. He'd had trouble with some new equipment Mr Verney had installed, and he kept muttering on about new-fangled nonsense.

In the end Jacob got up and said he thought he'd go for a pint at the Woolpack. I began to say, 'I'll come with thee, lad,' but as bad luck would have it, our Peggy set up a cry just then. I hurried up to her. She was teething. It's always a bad time for the little ones.

By the time I got back downstairs again, Jacob was gone. I considered going after him but then I realised he wouldn't like that. So I sat down with my darning and half-listened to my father complaining about the new weighing equipment.

I waited up for Jacob to come home. Peggy was wakeful for a time so I had a reason to put forward if he was annoyed. By and by she settled down at last. It was after midnight. Tired out, I went to bed and I suppose I slept heavily.

Next morning when the alarm went off I found Jacob was already up. I knocked on Dad's door and went down to make sure the tea was made and so on. I found our Jack in the kitchen crawling about under the table, playing pirates. It was quite usual to find him already up when I got downstairs but he generally amused himself without being a nuisance so I never insisted he must wait to be called.

Jacob hadn't made the tea yet. I put the kettle on and called up to my father.

'I'm coming, I'm coming!' he replied in annoyance. When he appeared he accepted his tea without comment for a time, then glanced about. 'Jacob had his?'

'Nay, he must have gone out to the barn first.'

'Owt wrong there?'

'Not that I know on.'

'Hmm . . . ' He put his tea down and went out.

Jack said, 'Are you making the toast now, Ma?'

'Just going to. Hungry, are you?' I sliced the bread and put it in front of the fire on the toaster. 'You watch it for me, will you?'

'Aye, I'll watch it, Ma.'

My father came hurrying in. 'He's not in the barn, Annie.'

'What?'

'He's not there. And t'vans's gone.'

I didn't know what to make of it. If Gran and her grandson had still been with us, Jacob might have driven over by the track to the far side of our land to pick Gippo up for the day's work. And any road, Jacob wouldn't set out to fetch Gippo without even a cup of tea. It seemed to me he wouldn't go anywhere of a morning without even a cup of tea.

The toast began to brown. Our Jack, who was giving it his full attention, turned it in the holder. Dad sat down and picked up his half-empty tea mug. 'What's to do, lass? Did he say owt to you about going anywhere first thing s'morning?'

'No, not a word.'

'Could he have set out betimes to get to a market some way off? What's on today . . . ?'

'Chelford? Wigton?'

'But why's he gone off there without telling us?'

'I don't know, Dad. And as far as I could gather, he hadn't made his mind to buy anything as yet. Unless he decided all of a sudden, he's no reason to go to market.'

'Gone up to look at the sheep, happen?'

'Aye. That might be it.' I felt a surge of relief.

'But that still doesn't explain why he's gone without saying so. And no breakfast?'

'It's a mystery.'

Dad ate up his breakfast and went to start his day at Verney's. He came hurrying back within about an hour. 'Annie! Mr Verney asked me what the Emmerdale Farm van was doing standing on the forecourt of Hotten Station!'

'At Hotten?' I repeated. 'How does he know?'

'Saw 'un. He drove into Hotten early this morning to collect a parcel off the mail train, and saw our van.'

'Jacob's gone somewhere by train, then?'

'Looks like it. But where? Why?'

I shook my head. A thought struck me. I went upstairs. I could hear our Peggy in her cot, making a singing sound of contentment to herself. In a minute it would be time to get her up and start her day. Our Jack was out playing in the garden, waiting for school time.

I looked in the wardrobe. Jacob's best suit was gone. So was the suitcase – we only had one. I looked in the drawers; he'd taken a change of shirt and socks and underwear.

When I told Dad, he gaped at me. 'He can't have gone off without a word!'

'Happen he left a note.' But though we searched everywhere we couldn't find one. It wasn't behind the mantlepiece clock, or propped up against the bread crock, or the tea caddy, or any of the likely places.

It was bewildering, frightening. But what made it worse was the news that came later in the day.

Emily Tewkesbury had packed up last night, said goodbye to Mrs Annersley after giving her a week's money in lieu of notice, and left Beckindale.

9

CHAPTER TEN

AT MY INSISTENCE, the van was left at Hotten Station until
next day. I was so certain Jacob had just gone away for
overnight on some idea of his that I felt he'd expect it to be
there next morning so he could drive home. But in the
evening of the following day I gave David Annersley our
spare set of keys and he took the bus to Hotten to bring the
van back.

'I – er – had a word with the booking clerk,' he said. In
those days, when Hotten still had a station and a train service, there was always staff on duty while the trains were
running. The booking clerk had been in his little cubby hole
when the milk train came through, and the mail train, and
the newspaper train.

What the booking clerk had to tell us wasn't very helpful.
A dark young man who answered Jacob's description had
bought a ticket to Leeds the previous morning, and boarded

the train.

Leeds? Why would he go to Leeds?

'Well . . . er . . . where has Emily gone, do you think?' David muttered.

'She doesn't live in Leeds, does she?'

'No. Ma has a home address for her. It's Salford.'

'That doesn't get us very far.'

'I . . . I think Emily's on the telephone at home. Would you like me to ring her there?'

I frowned at David. 'What reason could you give?'

'Oh, well, I'd think of something.'

I didn't say yes or no to that idea, but he went on with it on his own and reported back to me. 'Emily's not with her family. Her mother says she's gone to London.'

'London!'

'She's got an exhibition coming on there, if I remember right.'

'Yes.'

The gossips weren't slow to put two and two together. Jacob had gone missing from his home at the same time as Emily Tewkesbury had packed up and left.

Dad was so angry he could hardly speak of it. 'It's outrageous! He's a married man with two bairns!'

'Dad, there's no proof that they've gone away together. Or if they have, that there's anything wrong in it.'

'What are you saying? Nowt wrong in it?'

'I spoke to Emily on the morning of that day. She assured me that all she and Jacob ever did was chat.'

'And you believed her?'

'Of course I did.'

'Good heavens, girl, do you expect her to admit she was having a torrid affair with your husband?'

'Well . . . I think she's a very honest person. I don't think she'd say they just talked, if there was more to it.'

'Eeh, Annie,' Dad said. 'You always want to think the best of everybody – but this time it's got to be faced.'

After that first outburst, he was the soul of tact and gentleness to me. And I must say that most folk were careful not to say anything that could hurt me. But it's bitter to be the object of pity; I found it hard to bear.

Mr Verney stopped me in Beckindale High Street one morning a few days later. 'Any news?' he said with grave politeness.

'I'm afraid not.'

'I . . . don't wish to intrude. But if you have any news I'd be glad to hear.'

'Of course, Mr Verney.' It was natural he should be concerned. Jacob was his tenant. As a careful landlord, George Verney didn't want one of his farms left without a farmer to run it.

'I was in the Woolpack for a pint last night,' he went on, looking a little embarrassed. He felt it his duty to put in an appearance at the local about once in a month, to 'mingle' with the villagers. Not that it really worked. Most folk were too embarrassed by his presence to let themselves go. 'I heard it said that Miss Tewkesbury has gone to London?'

'Yes, Mr Verney.'

'I suppose you've no idea if that's where your husband has gone?'

'Last we heard, he'd gone to Leeds.' I realised Mr Verney wanted to find out if the gossip was true, if my Jacob had run off with Emily, as Mr Verney had had rather an eye to Emily himself.

'Yes, that was what they were saying. Only, they mentioned that he and Emily had a long serious talk the night she packed up and left.'

'They did?' I sighed. 'Well, folk are entitled to talk. "That's what makes mankind different from the rest of the animal kingdom – we can talk to each other".' I was quoting Emily, but Mr Verney wasn't to know that. He looked at me in surprise. 'I'm sorry,' I said. 'There's been a lot of "talk" one way and another. I wish folk would be more tolerant.'

'No one's been intolerant to you, Mrs Sugden, I'm sure.'

'Nay, I don't say that. It's tolerance for my Jacob I'm hoping for.'

The one person who talked in open terms about the situation was the vicar, Mr Harper. He came to see me with the object of offering his help. 'I've no intention of offering charity,' he said, 'but it seems to me you may be in difficulties over money. If there's anything you need I hope you'll let me know. There is a parish benevolent fund, remember.'

'But that's for old folk –'

'Not a bit. There's no rule that says so. It's not a big fund, of course, but it might be able to extend some help to tide you over.'

'Thank you, vicar. You're very kind.'

'Not a bit! If you want to know, I'm hopping mad! It's my duty as a Christian to think well of your husband, Mrs Sugden, but I find it very difficult.'

'Happen he's not entirely to blame,' I sighed. 'I feel I must have failed him somehow . . .'

'I shouldn't reproach yourself. No matter what failures there may have been – and none of us are a hundred per cent at human relationships – nothing can justify your husband's going away without even talking to you about the problems.'

'Vicar, it may be my fault that the crisis came that way. I'd lectured Emily about how she was harming my Jacob by letting him build castles in the air, so I think for that reason she decided to go. Happen, when she told Jacob, he couldn't bear it any more – the idea of having nobody to share his hopes and dreams . . .'

'That doesn't excuse him. He's been thoughtless, almost heartless! Really, Mrs Sugden, if I had him here I'd give him the rough side of my tongue –'

'What about forgiveness, Mr Harper?'

'Oh, us Christians have an example of misdeeds getting their instant reprisal! Remember Our Lord in the temple? I don't think righteous anger is entirely excluded – so long as we get the better of it afterwards. I'd be prepared to forgive Jacob if *he'd* forgive me for berating him. But it's not *my* forgiveness that's important. It's yours. You'd be prepared to forgive and forget? If . . . when . . . he comes back?'

'Let's say when, vicar. *When* he comes back.'

'You're as sure as that?'

'Well, I look at it this way. If he's gone off with Emily, I can't see what they've got in common. Her mother says she's gone to London over this painting show – Jacob knows nowt about painting, really, and he doesn't like cities for more than a little while. So unless there was a tremendous emotional tie, I can't think what would keep him there – and I have a feeling they weren't bound up in one another in that way.'

Mr Harper paced about my kitchen, looking perturbed. 'I wonder if you know how difficult it would be to live with a husband who's had to be "forgiven"? Your Jacob never struck me as an easy man at the best of times.'

'We'll deal with all that when time comes.'

'Sufficient unto the day is the evil thereof, eh? You're right, Mrs Sugden. But don't forget – if there's anything I can do. Anything – I mean it. My wife would be happy to babysit for you if you have to go . . . anywhere. To town, for instance.'

'Yes. Thank you.'

He took my hand at parting. 'You're one of those who believes in prayer, like me?'

'Yes, vicar.'

'Then I hope it's some help to know I'm praying for you, Mrs Sugden.'

I felt my throat go tight with tears that I could never shed in front of anyone. 'It is a help, vicar. I'm grateful.'

When I turn the pages of my diary for those days I see it's full of totally practical matters – sums worked out in some detail about how to manage. Money was difficult, to say the least. My father's wages from Verney's were our only income for day to day expenses.

Oh, I could have bought on credit at the village shop. But I've never been one for that. I always pay my way. I was brought up like that.

But, as days went into weeks, I had to think about more than the grocery bill. I had to start thinking about how to manage the farm.

Rent was paid up till 1st January in the next year. It was now October. I couldn't just sit and do nothing between now and then. I had to make up my mind whether to plant winter barley, for instance. If I was going to do that, it meant I was looking ahead to the use of the crop as feed for the following year. It meant I thought we'd still be here next year.

We had good barley in the sack in our barns, which would have helped to feed the milk herd in the coming months when the pasture grew thin. We had no herd. If I planted barley to be harvested next year, I was making a kind of promise that we were going to have a herd. Otherwise it was pointless – Emmerdale didn't have enough arable land to make grain crops worth the growing for sale.

All the time I was busy about the house or feeding the poultry, I was mulling over in my mind what was best to do. I reviewed the situation time and again.

The farm had no stock except the sheep on the uplands. There's little current income to be made from sheep unless you do it properly; the profit from the sale of the wool on a small herd isn't significant, not like the milk cheque from a milk herd.

So if we were going to go on, we had to have cows.

But that meant having staff to milk. My father would always lend a hand, but he was actually employed by Mr Verney. So he could only be considered very part-time.

I knew Gippo and Grannie Lee would be back by and by, but for the moment I'd no idea where they were. There were the neighbours: I knew I could always rely on a helping hand from old Mr Jamieson, and at a pinch Jim Gimbel would come, but he had more on his plate than Mr Jamieson so it wasn't fair to turn to him.

The most easily available help came from David Annersley. From the outset he'd put himself at my service, to act as chauffeur. I couldn't drive, so if anything had to be taken about in the van, David leapt to attention. He wasn't a farmer, but he was country-bred and knew how to milk and how to drive a tractor and how to dip a sheep.

One morning in the middle of October I woke up with a plan all ready in my head. I hadn't reached it consciously. It just presented itself and I knew that was what I had to do.

I'd decided to sell some sheep and with the money buy some cows.

Because of the foot-and-mouth outbreak, the demand for meat had been satisfied by lamb and mutton. Prices for lamb were very good. Conversely, because so many cattle had been slaughtered, replacement beasts were greatly in demand and their price, too, was high. I knew I wasn't going to get a complete herd for what I earned with the ewes and lambs; but I'd buy the best I could, and I'd decided on trying for Ayrshires.

I put this before my father as a settled plan. He pulled his chin, thought a minute, then said, 'Well, I can't see why not. Whether you go on here, or whether you have to sell up and go, it can't be a bad thing to have a milk herd.'

'I'm not leaving here, Dad.'

'But the farm's in Jacob's name, lass.'

'If worst comes to worst, I'm sure Mr Verney would transfer the tenancy to me.'

I wasn't by any means sure of that! Mr Verney was a conservative sort of estate owner and didn't let out his farms to women. But I was going to behave as if he would. I didn't see what else to do. And one thing I was determined on – I was going on at Emmerdale, with or without a husband.

On Dad's day off, and with help from David and Mr Jamieson, we separated out the best of our ewes with lambs. At that time we had black-faced sheep and it had always been my view that we ought to cross-breed them with a better ram; but Jacob had little interest in sheep. It's funny, when I look back now. In the present time, under Matt's guidance, we've got our flock up to prize-winning level. In the time I'm speaking of, our sheep were a haphazard lot. But still there were some strong ewes there, with good healthy lambs beside them.

David got a self-drive hire lorry and we took the ewes

with lambs to market. We did surprisingly well. But all I got for the money when I went to the cattle ring was six dairy cattle. I need hardly say, not accredited cows. We had no ambitions of that kind until our Joe got going years later.

We took the cows home and turned them out into the field nearest the house. The grass wasn't very good; the year had been too dry. And of course, due to the upset, their milk yield went down to nothing, although I'd made sure they were beasts who were late-calving. But before seven days had gone by, they'd settled down and we'd got full churns to put out for collection.

David was with us early and late. Now that the first embarrassment about Jacob's going had passed over, David was his usual cheerful self again. He tackled everything with a will.

'You shouldn't ought to accept so much help from him, Annie,' Dad said. 'Can't you see how it's beginning to look to everybody?'

I looked up from the mass of paperwork I was trying to put in order. 'Who else is there to help us, except David?' I challenged. 'Every farmer in the district has his own problems, trying to recover from the foot and mouth. David is the only man who's free to come to us – and I for one am grateful.'

'I think you're playing with fire,' he replied. He was genuinely worried. 'The lad has a feeling for you, Annie.'

'I know that. I like him too.'

'You're sure it isn't more than liking?'

'I'm sure, Dad. And now, please – let me have this time in peace to sort out these bills.'

My time for getting down to things like this was after the children were abed. I'd taken out all the papers in the drawer of the dresser and tried to put them in order. What worried me was that there were bills there, unpaid from a long way back, and with repeat notices and final notices muddled up among them. There was even a lawyer's letter from one firm, the firm from whom Jacob had bought last year's seed barley. I remembered now that he'd written a letter of complaint because of the low yield, and refused to pay the bill. I thought he was wrong, for the crop was of high quality though scant.

All this was muddled up with the host of leaflets and pamphlets which keep coming through the letterbox of every farmer. It took me one entire evening to sort out the Ministry's useful folders from the things sent by firms advertising weed control and feed additives and so on. Next evening I put the bills in order of importance to be paid. I planned to write to everybody and explain that there would be a delay, but that they'd get their money as soon as possible.

I can't abide the idea of being in debt. I always used to put aside a little sum out of the housekeeping each week for the coal and the paraffin, so that when the bill came in from the fuel man, I had it all ready. It would never have occurred to me to buy anything on hire purchase in those days, and even now I'm not keen on it – I always have to be sure in my own mind that I've got enough in the bank to pay for the goods if worst came to worst. To tell truth, the only reason I sometimes buy an item on hire purchase is because you get better maintenance service that way!

It was quite a shock to me to see how Jacob had let things slide. I'd always known there was a pile of paperwork in that drawer but I'd never taken him to task about it, because it was very much the rule in our house that the man dealt with all that kind of thing. It's still like that, to some extent. Joe runs the farm now, and though we have to have a vote on any big scheme, it wouldn't occur to any of us to interfere in his day-to-day decisions.

So I emptied the drawer on the kitchen table that first night with a feeling that I'd no right to do it – but I had no idea when Jacob might be back, and it was easy to guess that there were things there that needed attention. I hadn't expected unpaid bills going back to last year, though.

The total amount owed by the Sugdens, according to those invoices, was one hundred and eight pounds four shillings. That may not seem a lot today, but in those days it was a very great sum. The largest item was the bill for the barley seed which was twenty-two pounds. It was brought up rather high by the fact that they'd charged carriage extra; this was unusual, and seemed to mean they'd had trouble with Jacob before and didn't extend him the favour of 'carriage-paid'. The firm was a very good Yorkshire firm, Sorley's Feed and Grain Merchants.

I sat down after I'd got the bills in order, and wrote to Sorley's to tell them I would pay the bill in instalments if that would suit them. I put my letter in an envelope and stamped it. I intended to take it to the postbox in Beckendale next morning.

But before I could set out next day, a man came to the door of the farmhouse. 'Mr Sugden?'

'He's away at present,' I said. 'Can I do anything for you?'

'I'd like to speak to Mr Sugden himself.'

'That isn't possible, I'm afraid.'

'Look here, my dear,' this man said, pleasantly enough, 'tell him it's no use skulking in corners. He's got to come out one day.'

'Skulking? My husband isn't skulking!' I retorted. 'Who *are* you?

'Name's Vander, but that doesn't matter. I have to see your husband personally.'

'I've told you, you can't. He's gone.'

'Gone where?'

'To Leeds.'

'When will he be back?'

I hesitated. 'What's this about?'

'It's business, my dear. Important business.'

'Then you'll have to talk to me about it,' I said, bristling quite a lot under his patronising tone. 'My husband is away indefinitely and I'm in charge of the farm meanwhile.'

'You?'

'Why not, I'd like to know?'

He hesitated. 'Let's get this straight. You are running Emmerdale Farm?'

'I am. Ask anyone.'

He took a paper out of his pocket and looked at something typed on the outer fold of it. 'Emmerdale Farm,' he read. 'It's not personal to Mr Sugden after all, it seems. Right, my dear. There you are!'

He put the paper into my hand, tipped his hat, and walked back to his car.

'What is this?' I called, bewildered. 'Don't you want to wait for an answer?'

'You'll have to answer in court, my dear,' he said, and getting into his car, he drove off.

I looked at the paper in my hand. After a moment I unfolded it.

I'd been served with a summons to appear in court over the non-payment of the bill to Sorley's.

CHAPTER ELEVEN

I WON'T TELL you what my father said when I showed him the paper at dinner time. Even David, usually so cheerful, was struck speechless by it.

The court hearing was in two days' time. I took advantage of Mr Harper's kind offer to have his wife babysit for me. David drove me into Hotten in the van and accompanied me into court. We had to wait in the lobby until my name was called.

The magistrate was Mr Lofts, a well-known local man. He favoured an informal method of running his court. I think he must have seen how much I coloured up when the complaint was read, so he spoke rather gently to me.

'Why isn't your husband here to answer this complaint, Mrs Sugden?'

'He's away from home at the moment,' I said.

'But didn't you let him know there was a summons? It's

his place to answer it, not yours.'

'If you please, sir, I . . . I don't know how to get in touch with him at the moment.'

'Don't know how to get in touch? What d'you mean?'

'He's – he went away about a month ago, Mr Lofts. He –'

'Address the bench as your honour,' the clerk of the court put in in a shocked tone.

'Tush, tush, Mr Hayward, I don't mind what the young lady calls me so long as we get to the bottom of this matter.' Mr Lofts took off his specs and studied me. 'Your husband has gone away?'

'Yes, your honour.

'And you don't know where he is?'

'Not exactly, your honour.'

I could feel myself going even redder. This experienced man understood perfectly well that I was trying not to admit that my husband had left me, abandoned me.

'Hm . . .' he murmured. 'Did you know this bill was unpaid?'

'No, your honour. I got all the paperwork concerning the farm out of the dresser the other night and went through it, and I actually wrote to the firm promising to clear up the debt as soon as I could. But before I could post the letter, the bailiff handed me the summons.' I took it out of my handbag.

'Your honour,' put in the solicitor dealing with the case for Sorley's, 'it's quite easy for Mrs Sugden to produce a letter and claim she wrote it before the summons came.'

'Quite easy, Mr Desoto. But why should she, if it isn't so?'

'To create a favourable impression, your honour.'

'Hm,' said Mr Lofts, looking at the lawyer with a very cool glance. 'Do you think I'm easily impressed, Mr Desoto?'

This caused a little ripple of laughter, and Mr Desoto subsided.

'Now, young lady, let me see the letter.' He took it, opened it, and read it. 'You were offering to pay in instalments?'

'Yes, sir.'

'At what rate?'

'Well, I . . . I was going to have to ask for time to work that out. You see, your honour, we were wiped out by the foot-and-mouth, and my husband's gone as I've just explained—'

'You said you'd no idea where?'

'I didn't quite say that, sir. I think he's gone to London, probably, to try to raise the money to start again.'

'That seems reasonable. Has he much chance of raising the money?'

'Well, he tried in this neighbourhood a while ago. There's this scheme for improving hill land if you can put up your half of the cost – the government pays the rest.'

'Yes, I know of that, Mrs Sugden. Go on.'

'I think,' I said, and I really believed it while I said it, 'that my husband's gone to try and find someone who'll lend him the money to get the grant.'

'In London?'

'Well, there's lots of finance houses in London.'

'There are indeed. You haven't heard what success he's had?'

'Not yet, your honour.'

'In the meantime, you're managing the farm, I think you told the baliff.'

'Yes, sir.'

'Hm . . . You haven't the money available to pay this bill? Are you paying your farmhands their wages?'

I shook my head. 'We don't have any farmhands, Mr Lofts.'

'None?' He frowned at me. 'Come come, you can't manage a farm on your own, without help.'

'I didn't say I had no help. My father, who lives with us, does what he can in his spare time. He's an experienced stockman. And a friend, Mr Annersley, is being very kind and doing much of the work.'

'When you say 'doing much' – what does that entail? I

understand all your livestock was wiped out in the foot-and-mouth outbreak?'

'Not entirely, your honour. Most of our sheep were on the upper dale so Mr Riceyman let them go along while he kept an eye on them, and in fact they never showed any signs and weren't destroyed because there'd been no contact with sick animals.' I paused, feeling self-conscious at talking so much.

'Go on,' Mr Lofts encouraged.

'Well, sir, about a week ago I sold some sheep and bought some milking cows.'

'Indeed?' he frowned. 'How many?'

'Six, your honour.'

'Oh.' He let his gaze lighten. 'Hardly a vast investment. Nevertheless, if you've sheep to sell, couldn't you now sell more and pay this bill.?'

'Well, sir . . . fact is, I sold the best of them. I shouldn't like to try to foist what's left on the market. We haven't worked with our sheep enough. I'd feel badly about putting them into a sale – they'd fetch next to nowt and they wouldn't be a good bargain at that to whoever bought 'em.'

'Well,' Mr Lofts said, 'that's honest enough, at any rate!'

'If I could just say, sir . . . I didn't know there was this urgent bill when I sold the sheep. It was only after I'd done summat about making a new start with a milking herd as a source of a bit of income, that I got down to the bills in the dresser drawer. If I'd done it t'other way round, I wouldn't have bought the milkers, happen.'

'Hm . . . What's your plan now, Mrs Sugden? What do you intend for the future?'

'That rests with my husband, your honour. As soon as he's back, I guarantee he'll take steps to settle outstanding bills.'

'But meanwhile? You must agree, Sorley's have been very long-suffering. They deserve to have their money.'

'I agree, your honour.' I was at a loss. 'I don't know what to suggest. All I can say is, there was never any intention of not paying. Soon's we've got the money, we'll pay the bill.'

'Could you pay at a certain amount each week?'

I hesitated. 'It could only be a small amount, Mr Lofts. At the moment the money coming in is only what we get from the milk, and my father's wages . . . If we sell the cows to pay the bill, then we lose the milk cheque.'

'As to that . . . Can't you pay from the bank account? There *is* a bank account, I take it?'

'Yes, your honour. But the account's in my husband's name. I spoke to the bank manager and he says he can only accept my man's signature, not mine.'

'It isn't a joint account?'

'No, your honour.'

'Then how, may I ask, are you helped by having a cheque for the milk? Doesn't that go into the account?'

'Well . . . the village shop has agreed to cash the cheque for us. The cheque's made out to Emmerdale Farm so I'll endorse it on the back. Mrs Malton at the shop says she doesn't think there'll be any problem, from *her* bank. Milk Marketing Board's cheque is acceptable anywhere, really, isn't it?'

Mr Lofts took out a handkerchief and began to clean his specs. 'You've certainly had problems getting enough to get by on,' he remarked.

'Oh, it's all right, your honour. Farming folk are used to cash problems.'

'Mr Desoto?' the magistrate said, with a little gesture towards Sorley's lawyer.

'Yes, your honour.' Mr Desoto got up. 'I think I can safely say that my clients wouldn't wish to add to the problems of this worthy young lady. But they *are* entitled to their money.'

'Quite so. They've waited a long while so far. Would they be prepared to wait until Mrs Sugden's husband returns?'

'If we could have some idea, your honour, when that is likely to be . . .?'

Mr Lofts turned his glance on me. 'Mrs Sugden?'

'Any day now, sir,' I said. I kept saying this to myself; no matter what other folk might believe, I always told myself

10

each morning that Jacob would be back.

The magistrate leaned back, put on his glasses, and stared at the ceiling. Then he said, 'I think I will adjourn this case without a date for a further hearing. Perhaps, Mr Desoto, you will ask your clients to allow Mrs Sugden further time. Let's say . . . where are we now . . . end of October. Let's say we think about this again in the New Year. If Mr Sugden hasn't taken steps to clear up his debt by then, you will bring the matter back to court. Will you go along with that?'

Mr Desoto turned to a gentleman sitting in the row behind him and had a little conference. It dawned on me that this gentleman was from Sorley's.

'Well, Mr Desoto?'

'My client is agreeable to that. The firm don't want it to be thought that they are unfeeling towards farmers, particularly in a year like this one when there's been so much hardship.'

'That's generous, Mr Desoto. Very well then . . . adjourned *sine die*. That's all, I think, Mrs Sugden. You may step down.'

'Excuse me, your honour, what exactly does it mean?'

'It means you can go. Sorley's will wait for their money. But I must ask you to speak to your husband as soon as he gets back or gets in touch, and tell him that he's left his affairs in a most unsatisfactory state, even if only temporarily. No doubt it's an oversight. But he ought to have made arrangements for you to draw money from his account.'

'Yes, sir. I'm afraid he's been a bit put about by all the troubles that came with the foot-and-mouth.'

'No doubt. It's been a trying time. Very well, Mrs Sugden, we'll leave it at that. Good luck.'

'Thank you, your honour.'

I was so relieved that I couldn't speak. Even when David congratulated me I didn't do anything but nod. On the way home to Emmerdale I just listened to his cheerful chat about the case as he'd heard it from the public benches – he seemed to think it had been quite a triumph for me, but I don't know how. Having to talk about your private life in public is awful.

Dad was as relieved as I was when I told him the news. Even more so when I reported that there had been hardly anyone in court. 'Thank goodness for that,' he said. 'Had up in court! What are we coming to?'

But if we thought we'd escaped public notice, we were wrong. We'd forgotten the local paper.

The report was about half a column and it had a little headline: 'Farmer's Wife Holds the Fort'. It began: 'Farmer Jacob Sugden's trip to London in search of finance for a farm improvement scheme has left his wife in a fix. This was explained in Hotten Magistrates' Court on Thursday when Mrs Sugden appeared in answer to a summons for debt.' It then went on to tell, quite fairly, what had happened and ended with unexpected kindness: 'Good luck to Mr Sugden in his search for scarce resources to put his farm in order. We all know the problems facing farmers this year end, don't we . . .'

My father went beetroot-red as he put the paper down. 'Well', he groaned, 'we'll never be able to hold up our heads again.'

'Don't be silly, Dad. It doesn't matter.'

'It matters to *me* .'

It mattered to me, too, but I wasn't going to admit it. I wanted to put it behind me and get on with the business of running Emmerdale.

It was strange, that back-end of the year. Everybody else in the country was looking forward to the Coronation, which was to be in June of the following year. There was a lot of talk in the newspapers and magazines about the New Elizabethan Age, and fashion became very important – there were sketches of the gowns the ladies were going to wear for the ceremony and of course all the fashion houses hoped to sell clothes for the parties and balls that would follow.

It all seemed to be happening in another world from the one I lived in. Mine was a world where you wore clothes to keep out the cold and to protect yourself against damage by thorns and twigs.

Mind you, I'm not claiming that us farmers were the only ones who'd had hard times. There was a terrible flood in Lynmouth in Devon in the early part of that year, and then in the beginning of the month when I had to go to court, there had been a dreadful railway disaster near London – over a hundred people were killed. I kept reminding myself that, no matter what a coil I was in, at least I had my two children safe and sound, and my father still with me to lend a hand. He was quite fit, except that he had a bit of trouble with his chest as the colder weather came on. When, in early December, there was an absolutely killing fog in London that cost hundreds of lives among bronchitis sufferers, I tried to persuade him to take more care of himself. 'If you'd just give up your pipe, Dad . . .'

'Huh,' he'd grunt. 'Nobody's proved to me that smoking a pipe does you any harm.'

And really, he had so few pleasures apart from his pipe and an occasional pint, I didn't like to nag him about it.

The time was coming when I'd have to decide what to do about the seed barley. Was I going to sow it or not? It was December; winter barley has to go in before the turn of the year, because part of the growing process for that variety is to have the frost in the ground. It causes what's called 'tillering', causing the root to split up as it forms so that you get more than one stem from each seed. There's no point in planting the seed of winter-barley in the spring; it should go in during late autumn to have the cold months to develop.

If I decided to plant it, I'd have to ask David to drive the tractor for the drill. I was unwilling to do it. I was indebted to him enough. I ought to have paid him wages for his help with the milking, though he always refused the idea – but if I got him to drive the tractor for me I ought to make him a member of the farm staff and all that, so that he was insured against accident.

I let the problem simmer in my mind for almost a week. Then one evening I said to Dad: 'What do you think about the barley, Dad?'

'You ought to sow,' he said at once. 'No matter what, you're going to have to feed stock. You can't use those fields more profitably than barley.'

He was taking about our ley lands, which had yielded grass that summer. Jacob had ploughed after the hay harvest. There they were – empty fields waiting to be used.

'I think I'll see about hiring the seed drill in the morning,' I said.

He nodded. 'No problem there. Everybody else in the district is finished with sowing by now.'

'Well, we're late, that's all there is about it.'

'Have Seed Cut on our land next year, happen.'

'Aye.'

Neither of us said what was in our mind: Would Jacob be here to see the barley in the ear? Would he be there if the Seed Cut was at Emmerdale in the autumn?

Before I went to bed, I went into the children's room as I always did, to make sure they were all right. Peggy was sweetly asleep, but something about our Jack's breathing told me he was awake. I said: 'You all right, lad?'

He sat up. 'Ma, Dinah Soames is going to Leeds to the panto on Boxing Day. Ma, she says her Ma would take me too if I could pay for my ticket and the train fare. Ma, can I go?'

I sat down on the end of his bed. 'We can't afford it, Jack.'

He pulled up his knees and sat, hugging them. 'How is it Mrs Soames can afford it, Ma? Is it because Mr Soames isn't away?'

'That helps, lad.'

'Why doesn't our Dad come back, then?'

'He'll be back when it's time, son. Don't thee fret.'

'Will he be back in time for the panto?'

'We'll see,' I said, stifling a sigh.

I should have replied 'yes' to his question. Because next morning, as I was setting out for Beckindale to ask if the seed drill was available from the farmer's co-operative, my Jacob walked in.

CHAPTER TWELVE

HE SET DOWN his suitcase just inside the door. 'Got your coat
on, I see,' he said. 'Going out?'

I swallowed hard. 'I was going to see if I could get the use of
the seed drill.'

'Oh? What for?'

'Barley.'

'Aye, it should be in by now.'

I didn't say, 'And would have been, if you'd been here!'
Instead I unfastened my coat. 'Had breakfast?'

'I had a sandwich at the transport cafe with the chap who
gave me a lift.'

'Cup of tea, then?'

'Aye, that'd be grand.'

He sat down. I busied myself with the kettle and the teapot.
He said nothing.

'Came back by lorry, then?'

'Aye, got a lift all the way from Watford By-Pass.'

'Watford. Near London, is that?'

He nodded. I put his tea in front of him, and the sugar bowl. He stirred vigorously then said, 'I heard cows in the back pasture?'

'Aye, they're still out though grass is thin.'

'How many?'

'Six. I sold the best of the sheep for them.'

'I see. That makes sense.'

'I'm glad you think so.' That wasn't said to challenge him. I was genuinely glad he approved. After all, this was his farm.

'Who's been milking?'

'Me and Dad and David Annersley.'

'Gran and Gippo not back yet?'

'Nay, they're still travelling. I expect they'll come when the weather hardens.'

He drank his tea. 'What're you paying David?'

'Nowt, so far, just his meals. But if I'd got him to sow t'barley, I'd have paid him a wage.'

'No need now. I'll see to it.'

'Aye.'

'Best get those cows indoors before the end o' the month. The weather forecast is bad for t'winter.'

'Aye. Only thing is, Jacob . . . we've only got limited feed. and no cash to buy in anything.'

'We can get it on credit.'

I shook my head. 'Better not, lad. We had a bit o' trouble over the bill to Sorley's.'

'Sorley's?'

'Last year's seed barley. The bill was never paid.'

He sighed. 'I meant to pay it. I just kept putting it off.' Then he looked up. 'You paid it, though?'

'I couldn't. T'bank wouldn't accept my signature.'

A look of utter horror crept over his face. 'What?'

'Mr Attcroft said he'd make some arrangement if you hadn't come back by the end of six months – open an account for me, in my own name, I s'pose.'

'You mean you haven't been able to draw money?'

'No, lad. Not a penny.'

'Annie!' He sprang up, sending his tea mug flying. 'What the devil d'you mean? How have you been managing?'

'Dad's wages – and the cheque for the milk now we've got six cows.'

'But . . . but . . . For Pete's sake, Annie! I took it for granted Attcroft would make the account open to you!'

'Nay, Jacob, it's against banking principles.'

'Banking principles! Damn the man! Was he going to let you starve before he let you have money you were entitled to?'

'There was no question of that, lad. We would have managed somehow. Only . . . it was difficult to know what to do about the farm. Time was getting on, and it seemed to me decision had to be made. So that's why I started again with the milk herd. I bought Ayrshires. What d'you think?'

'Oh, they're all right. On this trip, I've seen a lot of different dairy cattle.'

'In London?' I remarked, mopping up the spilt tea.

'Well, Smithfield Show's in London, tha knows, lass.'

I let a moment go by. 'But Smithfield was the early part o' this month. It was September when tha left, lad.'

'Well, there were a great fog i' London – you must have heard. Cattle at show were poorly. I stayed to lend a hand wi' them. Then I've been to the Dairy Show at Olympia and the Westmorland Show – seen a lot, I have.'

I went to the sink, rinsed the cloth, and hung it over the front of the draining board. 'Did Emily enjoy it?'

'Emily?'

'Emily Tewkesbury.'

'What on earth has she got to do with it?'

I sighed. 'That's what everybody's asking, lad. She left the same day you did.'

'I know that. But she went to see about her one-man painting show, as I recall. I went to look at the agricultural shows.'

'Oh, you did? I wish you'd let us know.'

'What?' He was staring at me, clearly baffled.

'You've been gone nigh on three months. We'd no notion

where you were or what you were doing.'

'Of course you knew.'

'No we didn't

'Yes you did.'

'How could I know, Jacob? You just walked out.'

'Walked out?'

'Before the rest of us were stirring. You just vanished.'

'I did nothing of the sort!'

'What d'you mean? One day you were there, next morning you had vanished.

'I didn't vanish!' he said hotly. 'I told you I was going, what I was planning.'

'Told me?' I shook my head, worried about him. 'You know you never said a word, love.'

'I didn't *say* it. I'm not saying I said it in so many words. But it was in my note.'

'What?'

'In my note. I explained what I was going to do.'

'What note?'

'The one I left on the kitchen table.'

'There was no note, Jacob.'

'Of course there was!'

'No, love.'

'But I wrote you a note!' he protested, his voice rising. 'I sat down and wrote it before I went out the door.'

'No.'

'Annie, I left it in the middle of the kitchen table.'

I was going to tell him that we'd searched everywhere and found nothing, when it dawned on me that it wouldn't help matters. If he wanted to believe he'd written a note, perhaps it was better to leave it be. I freely admit that at the moment I didn't believe his story.

But months afterwards, when I was tidying out our Jack's toy box, I found the note. Our Jack had used it as a sail for his toy boat. I remember he was playing pirates under the kitchen table that morning, and pushing his boat along the floor. Gippo had made the boat for him – it was a plain little thing with a mast in the middle and there had been sails originally, stitched by Gran. But at some time Jack had taken them off.

I think I said that he was apt to get up before the rest of us in the morning. He must have started his game of pirates, needed a sail for the boat, found a piece of paper on the table with 'grown-up writing' on it that he couldn't read, and just pushed the paper on to the spit of wood that made the mast.

The note said: 'I feel I've got to have a bit of a break so I'm off to take a look at other folk's milk herds. Might be a week or two, longer, happen. Love, Jacob.'

But at that moment, I didn't know the note was crumpled up at the bottom of the toy box. All I wanted was to avoid a disagreement now that Jacob was back.

I couldn't help saying, 'You might have let us have a line from you, to know where you were.'

'Ah . . .' he shrugged. 'You know I'm not good at writing letters.'

'A postcard, then.'

He had the grace to look ashamed. 'I meant to,' he muttered. 'I never got around to it.'

If he'd just sent a postcard from the Westmorland Show! That was the one he must have gone to first, for it takes place in September. It would have let us know he'd gone in quite the opposite direction from Emily.

'Eh, lad,' I murmured. 'I've been right worried.'

'You must have been,' he acknowledged. 'I'm sorry, Annie. I'd no idea you hadn't had my note. I suppose I should have talked it over with you before I took the plunge. But . . . I dunno . . . that night, when I went to bed, I was so unsettled . . . I couldn't sleep.'

I couldn't help remembering that was the night Emily had probably told him she was leaving. But I said nothing about that.

'I got up about half-past-three,' he went on. 'I don't know that I was sure what I was going to do, even then. But after a bit I realised there was a train from Hotten at half-four, and I found I'd decided to go and catch it. So I packed a few things, wrote you a note, and drove off.'

'And you've been on the move all the time?'

'More or less. I got lifts when they were available and took the train at other times. I've seen a lot of farming,' he added with a little smile.

'And what have you decided?'

'I don't know that I've come to any decisions . . .' He accepted a fresh mug of tea and sat with it in his hands, warming his palms. 'It's money, you see, Annie. There's a lot that could be done if only we had the money.'

'That's true, lad, but we've got to manage with what we've got. There's still the compensation for the foot-and-mouth, isn't there? We ought to make a start with that. There's a lot of bills need paying, you know, Jacob. I sorted 'em out. It's a bit of a shock . . .'

'Oh . . . well . . . I'll pay them. I always meant to pay them.'

'But it's not fair to make folk wait.'

'They can afford it better than I can!'

I made no reply to that. I took my coat upstairs, to give us a little space for reflection. When I came back, he was rinsing his mug under the tap.

'You were going to get the barley sown, eh? I'll go and see about t'drill.'

'Aye, you do that.'

'Next week I think I'll go to Loudwick to see if I can find a few more milkers. Six isn't enough to be worthwhile.'

'Jacob . . .'

'What?'

'I think you should call on Mr Verney. He doesn't know you're back.'

'What's it to do wi' him?'

'Well . . . Rent day's coming soon. He . . . I think he was wondering if I'd be able to pay . . .'

'Oh, devil take it!' he burst out, irritated. 'Fancy anybody having notions like that. I was only away a few weeks!'

'It seemed a long time to us, Jacob.'

At that he paused, and came up to me. He put a finger under my chin and tilted my face up. 'I gave you a fright, didn't I?' he said. 'I'm sorry, love.'

'So long as you're back safe and sound . . .'

'Aye.' He gave me a little kiss, wheeled round, and hurried out.

I went into a whirl of activity once he was gone. I unpacked his suitcase and washed the contents—I saw to my surprise that he'd bought a new shirt and a pair of gloves. Then I busied myself cooking a special meal for midday—roast chicken with all the trimmings, and apple pie with cloves.

When Jack came home for dinner I told him his Dad had come back. He blinked at me with his dark eyes and then said, matter-of-factly, 'Can I go to the panto with Dinah, then?'

I began to laugh. 'Aye, Jack, I believe you can.'

Dad had seen Jacob at Verney's. He got home ahead of him, though, because Jacob had gone into Beckindale to book the seed drill. 'Hey, Annie, he's as cool as a cucumber about the whole thing!' he began. 'Seems to think he's done nowt wrong!'

'I hope you didn't start an argument with him.'

'I was so taken aback when he strolled in,' he admitted, 'I couldn't say a word'

'Thank goodness for that.'

'What about Emily Tewkesbury, then?'

'They were never with each other.' I took satisfaction in saying that.

He had the grace to look ashamed. 'Well, you must admit it looked right fishy.'

'Only if you wanted to think t'worst.'

He shrugged. 'I spoke to David Annersley on my way past their cottage.'

'You did? What did you say?'

'Said he didn't need to come back for afternoon milking now our Jacob was home.'

'Oh, Dad!'

'What's the matter now?'

'That's downright ungrateful!'

'Listen, lass, the sooner that was put an end to, the better.'

'But there was never anything in it—'

'Not on your side, happen. I'm not so sure about David.'

'Only if you wanted to think t'worst,' I said again.

'I don't think t'worst of David for liking you, lass. But it can't go on. And he ought to know it.'

'We could be friends with him, surely—'

'Better not, Annie, better not.'

It was amazing how quickly everything settled down to normal again. Jacob took over the handling of the 'dairy herd', soon adding to it by purchases he made at Loudwick Market. I made sure he paid the outstanding bills. He sowed the barley just before the cold weather closed in. Gran and Gippo turned up to get settled in time for Christmas. On January 1st, Jacob went to The Hall to drink a glass of 'lamb's wool' and eat a piece of pepper cake with Mr Verney and the rest of the tenants before they paid their annual rent.

Lamb's wool is a traditional Christmas drink with us. It's called by that name because apple pulp is floated on top of the punch to look like fleece.

Both farmers and wives got lamb's wool to drink. Then the menfolk would withdraw to the study, where they paid their rent and were given receipts. Meanwhile the wives exchanged gossip and drank more lamb's wool—sometimes they got quite merry! On that Quarter Day I was given a good few nudges and some inquiries about what my man had been up to all those weeks he was missing from home.

'He was making up his mind what kind of farm he wanted to have,' I said, trying to look unperturbed.

'And what kind of farm does he want?' they asked. 'One he won't have to work at?'

'He's got plans,' I said.

That was true enough. He still longed to improve the marshland that was so unprofitable. But he still had no idea how to raise the cash he would need before he could apply for the government grant.

His tour round the country had filled him with new ideas. He'd seen how other farmers tackled their problems, and come home eager to do as well as they did, or better. But he still didn't know *how*. As always, it was the practicalities that defeated him.

Our neighbours meant well, but their little jokes began to

irritate my man. He was taken aback when Mr Harper said a disapproving word about his absence, the first time we all went to church together after his return. But what really startled and angered him was the bank manager.

Jacob had decided to have another go at getting the money from the bank. He'd bought some good dairy cattle with the compensation money, so he thought he could point to them as guarantee that he was a good subject for a loan.

To his astonishment, Mr Attcroft turned him down flat.

He came home fuming. 'Told me I was irresponsible,' he raged. 'Irresponsible! Me, that's running a farm and building up a new herd –'

'You think you're thoroughly responsible, do you?' Dad broke in.

Dad had held his peace very well ever since Jacob came back. I'd begged him to think on, because we all had to live together. But this outburst of annoyance from Jacob was more than he could bide.

'Of course I'm responsible,' Jacob said, surprised.

Dad looked up to heaven. 'Man, man,' he said. 'No responsible person would walk out on his wife and children in the middle of the night without a word!'

'I didn't go without a word! I left a note!'

'You left a note!' My father flashed a glance at me. We'd agreed not to dispute this point although up till then we'd still never seen this famous note. 'So you think that's the way to behave, do you? Disappear for three months, leave a note, so-long-don't-expect-me-till-you-see-me? No arrangement made for upkeep? No right-thinking man would do a thing like that! Look around thee, lad, and tell me which of thy neighbours would do a thing like that!'

'Oh, them!' Jacob cried. 'They're all set like concrete –'

'Aye, and them's the kind bank managers lend money to! Tha canst *build* on concrete, lad!'

Jacob had just taken off his outdoor coat and sat down at the outset of this exchange. Now he got up and stormed out, without his coat.

'Jacob!' I cried. 'It's too cold out there –'

'Let him go, lass,' Dad said. 'Let him get froze! Might bring him to his senses.'

'Why did you do that?' I demanded. 'Didn't we promise each other not to reproach him?'

My father caught back the words on the tip of his tongue. He sighed, raised his shoulders and dropped them in admission of blame. 'I'm sorry. He got my goat. I've done my best, lass, but *someone's* got to bring home to him the error of his ways.'

'You'll only do harm that way. Jacob has to see things for himself. He'll never take it from anyone else.'

'Afore God, Annie, you're too long-suffering! Why don't you fly out at him?'

Why not? Because it wasn't my way. Happen that was a bad thing. Happen Jacob needed a wife that would be ready to take up the cudgels when he did things that were a bit thoughtless.

'I think I used up all my energy just managing to keep going while he was away,' I excused myself.

'But that's the point! He's got to be made to see what he did! You went through three months of misery—'

'Aye, but don't you understand, Dad? He was quite unaware of that. It's no good trying to make him feel guilty about it—he hasn't a notion that I was unhappy all that time.'

Unhappy was scarcely the word. To me his absence had been a disaster, a tragedy, even. To him, it had been an interesting twelve weeks of jaunting around the country, with the excuse that he was seeing how best to spend his compensa-·tion money. I'd come to understand that that was just a self-vindication; the fact was that Jacob had needed to get away, had reached his limit of endurance for some reason. I felt I'd played some part in pushing him to the decision by warning Emily off. Talking to Emily was a sort of escape-valve to him, and I'd shut it off. I'd acted for the best, but happen I'd made a mistake. Any road, I'd learned from that mistake. I wasn't going to push Jacob again – otherwise he might be off for another three months, and I didn't think I could bear that.

It was no good asking Dad to apologise for his remarks. But he tried to show by his manner that he wanted a peaceful life, and things settled down. But all the same it was worrying.

Jacob was still hoping and scheming for something he couldn't have, the grant to improve our marginal land.

Once I went to Leeds with the Women's Institute on a theatre outing. The play we saw was called *The Three Sisters*, and I suppose Mrs Jowett, the organiser, chose it because she thought it would be a nice family story. But in fact it was about these three lasses in nineteenth-century Russia, living in the country miles from anywhere and hating it (though I don't know why, because to me they didn't seem to have a bad life—but you know what Russians are like, all moods and depressions.) Any road, what I'm trying to say is, these girls used to sit around and sigh, 'If one could but go to Moscow!' They had convinced themselves that if they could move to Moscow, everything would be different.

When I saw that play, I thought of my Jacob. He had convinced himself that if he could set to work on that marshy land and bring it into arable cultivation, it would make everything different. He could grow more grain for sale, and with the profits he could buy better dairy cattle and improve the herd, and so on and so on. It was all quite true—but the only way to get to the starting point was to set-to, to earn the money to be eligible for the grant.

But that was the one thing he didn't seem able to do. I can't explain it. All I could do was live with it.

One morning in early February a letter came for me, in a fine envelope with a typewritten address. When I picked it up I couldn't imagine what it could be. Nobody wrote to me using a typewriter! I opened it, and found it was a letter from a firm of solicitors in Harrogate.

'Dear Mrs Sugden, Inquiries have ascertained that you are the Anne Sugden, great-niece of Angela Maria Halbert, whom we have been asked to find. If you would be so good as to call at our offices in Harrogate at some time convenient to yourself, I should be obliged. Yours faithfully, Thomas Lacey, Consultant.'

When I'd read that, I sank down on the nearest chair. Go and see a lawyer? Whatever for?

When Dad came home at dinner-time I showed him the

letter. Did he know an Angela Maria Halbert?

He frowned and shook his head. 'Never heard of her.'

'It says here I'm her great-niece.'

'Well, it's not on our side of the family, I can tell you that,' he said. 'None of the Pearsons married into a family called Halbert. Halbert? I never heard of them.'

Jacob's attitude was more intrigued. 'Go on, go and ring 'em up and see what they want. Why not?'

After I'd cleared up the dinner dishes I walked to the phone box in Beckindale to make the call. The young lady who replied wouldn't or couldn't tell me anything. All she'd do was ask me to make an appointment to see Mr Lacey, which I did – for the following day.

Jacob agreed to take charge of our Peg while I made the trip to Harrogate. I put on my good coat of Yorkshire tweed and my town shoes and carried my best handbag, the one I take to church on Sundays. Jacob gave it to me; it's real leather.

Mr Lacey rose to shake hands when I was shown in by the nice young woman in his outer office. 'Well, Mrs Sugden, this is a pleasure. It's taken some time to get in touch.'

'I . . . don't really understand this,' I said. 'We don't seem to know anybody called Halbert.'

'She was actually your great-great-aunt. The great-aunt of your mother. Your mother was the daughter of Arnold and Alice Thrapsby of Harrogate?'

'Yes, that's right.'

'Mrs Halbert was the aunt of Alice Thrapsby. She left Yorkshire in 1878 as a child – you realise that in days gone by, when families were far larger than they are now, it was quite common for an aunt to be younger than her own nieces and nephews . . .?'

'Well, yes . . .'

'Her parents took her to the United States where they took up land in Montana. They became apple farmers –'

'Apple farmers?'

'We would say they had an orchard,' Mr Lacey said, smiling. 'They did well and in fact sold out in the end to a "corporation" in the business of growing fruit. Mrs Halbert, as she now was, retired to Florida.'

'Oh yes?' I said, dazed.

'Yes,' he said, nodding. 'She died there two years ago aged ninety, leaving most of her money to charities, but there were certain bequests to relatives "to keep up family ties" as she phrased it. You were one of the legatees, Mrs Sugden – "any children or grandchildren of Arnold and Alice Thrapsby of Harrogate." You are the sole surviving grandchild of Arnold Thrapsby, music teacher and organist.'

'Good gracious.'

'And I have much pleasure in telling you that you have a nice little legacy coming to you. In fact, the sum of five hundred pounds.'

'*What*?'

'Five hundred pounds.'

'Left to me?'

'Not by name. "Any children or grandchildren . . ." That was how Mrs Halbert expressed it.'

'But . . . but . . . I never *heard* of Mrs Halbert!

'No, that's so, I know you haven't heard of her. She married in Montana, of course. Her family name was Swithin. Alice Thrapsby's mother's brother was a Swithin. Am I clear?'

'Not a bit,' I gasped. 'I've never been able to understand family trees. I'm not even sure that I remember what he said about it.

'Well, never mind. I assure you the research has been done.'

'But . . . I mean . . . is that right? That I should have money coming to me from a woman I never heard of?'

Mr Lacey looked at me with a solemn expression and took a moment before he replied. 'This is a perfectly legal sum of money which you are entitled to claim. I advise you to claim it.'

It had all come as such a shock I couldn't take it in. 'I really don't understand . . .'

'You're unusual, Mrs Sugden. Most people are only too eager to believe they have sums of money coming to them from long-lost relatives.'

'No offence,' I said. 'I'm not saying you haven't got it right. It just seems . . . I mean, why should she bother? If she left

Yorkshire in 1878 and hasn't bothered to be in touch since then?'

'Who can say? The human heart is strange.'

'Did she write to us? Is there a letter, or anything?'

Mr Lacey frowned. 'There are some legal documents,' he said.

'No personal message?'

'No. Quite the contrary.'

'How d'you mean?'

'This is to be a quite impersonal transaction, Mrs Sugden.'

'Oh yes, I know, legal matters are impersonal. I understand that.' Yet suddenly I looked at him. It was odd. I got the impression he was trying to keep this more impersonal than usual.

'It would have been nice to have some more human contact,' I said. 'Some idea of what she was like . . .'

'I can supply you with a cutting from the Florida Gazette announcing her death,' he offered, 'but it's merely the obituary.'

I took it. It was just the usual announcement: 'At the Sunny Palms Home . . .'

'A home?' I murmured.

'She was very old.'

'Of course. I just thought – it's amazing she had money to leave.'

'Well, there you are,' he said, looking a bit perturbed. Then, with a little smile, 'Newspapers are useful, aren't they? The record of daily life.'

'Yes.

'Now, as to the legacy. I have the papers here. Shall I call in my clerks to witness your signature?'

I hesitated. 'Can I go away and think about it?'

Mr Lacy looked taken aback. 'Think about it? Why should you do that?'

'I don't know if it's right to accept the money. She didn't know me at all.

'Mrs Sugden!'

The truth was, somehow I was uneasy about it. I persuaded

the solicitor I needed time to think about it and made for the door. Once there, I turned. 'Mr Lacey, you signed the letter with your name and after it you put 'Consultant'. What does that mean?'

He looked even more startled. 'Why . . . I . . . er . . . I'm a consultant on overseas legal matters.'

'Overseas?'

'Yes.' He seemed to recover. 'Law is different in various countries, as you can imagine. My role is to make sure everything runs smoothly when money is to come into this country.'

'I see. Is American law so different from British?'

'Different enough.'

'You deal with other countries too?'

'Yes.'

'Europe?'

'No, I don't deal with European law.' He paused. 'My speciality is the Americas, North and South.'

'I see. Thank you.'

Don't ask me why, but as I left I was certain in my mind that the money we'd just been discussing came, not from some dead relative, but from Laurence Stanton. I couldn't yet work out the why's and wherefore's, but I *knew*.

On the way home from Harrogate to Beckindale by train and bus, I gradually came to see how it had been done. It was the quip by Mr Lacey about the newspaper: the record of daily life.

I recalled that someone – I thought it was Laurence – had sent money to give the children of Beckindale a present at Festival of Britain time. I'd been sure then that he'd seen the picture of our Jack with the other, smarter children on the outing.

Now I was equally sure that Laurence had seen the report of the case at the magistrate's court, and was now trying to send help. Because he wanted to do good by stealth, he'd got this law firm in Harrogate to do some research and find a dead relative who might have left me some money – there had to be an excuse, otherwise he knew I'd not take it.

When I got back the men were already eating their tea; I'd left it all ready in the oven. They burst out with: 'Well? What was it about?'

As soon as I mentioned the name Swithin from among those I remembered, Dad threw up his hands. 'That's right! I remember your mother mentioning him. Rainy Swithin – some cousin or uncle or something. It's a funny name, isn't it?'

'How much is the legacy?' Jacob asked. 'When d'you get it?'

'There are papers and things,' I said, vague on purpose. 'Exchange problems, I daresay. Mrs Halbert died in America, remember.'

'Oh aye. You've got to go back, then?'

'Aye.'

They took it for granted I was going to accept the legacy. I didn't know what to say. I just let them talk round it all evening, exclaiming and wondering at it. Our Jack listened wide-eyed, and said: 'Have you come into a fortune, Ma?' I don't know where he got hold of that one!

'Nay,' I said. 'It's only a small sum, I reckon.'

When bedtime came, I lingered. Jacob said, 'Aren't tha comin' up, lass?'

'I'll see to t'fire,' I said. 'I want the oven ready for baking in t'morning.'

'Right.'

When I'd banked up the fire, I sat by the kitchen range and thought. I was wondering if I ought to accept the money.

I knew for sure that it came from Laurence. I might have had an Aunt Halbert but she hadn't left me anything. I didn't even know for sure she'd died recently – there'd been no date on the cutting Mr Lacey showed me.

Was it right to take money from a man you'd once been in love with? I'd had to accept the gift for our Jack but could I accept a sum of money? I was a married woman. I ought not to be receiving presents – lavish presents – from another man.

But, if you looked at it from Laurence's angle, it probably wasn't all that lavish. I had to remember that he was now the stepson of a very rich man. I've since then seen a magazine article about the rich in Argentina, and I realise they're really rich – not shabby genteel like a lot of our landowners, but with stacks of money. To me, five hundred pounds really was 'coming into a fortune'. To Laurence, it was probably neither here nor there.

Then there was the problem of how I'd account for it if I refused. I'd have to explain about Laurence. And I couldn't bring myself to talk about it.

Looking back now from middle age, I see I was getting myself in a state about nothing. I wasn't by any means the first girl who'd been in love and had to say goodbye. All the same, I think there are thousands of people with experiences in their lives that they never talk about, and I had never talked about Laurence. Even my mother never knew – and I was close to my mother.

I shrank from having to explain that I thought the money came from the boy I used to love during the war. I knew it would hurt Jacob to learn that there had been someone I'd cared for more than him. I knew it would rather shock my father. Nothing wrong had ever happened – nevertheless, Dad would think I ought not to have been as close as that to anyone except my husband.

Dear me, how I fretted and fussed myself that night, sitting by the fire! I wonder if Laurence, far off on the other side of the ocean, could sense how unhappy I was?

When at last I went to bed, I'd made my decision. I'd sign the papers and take the money. In the first place, it would hurt Laurence if I refused – and I didn't want to hurt him. In the second place, it would relieve me of the need to explain a refusal. Thirdly and by no means least – it would help Jacob.

With that money, we could pay off all our debts and get that government grant. More than that, it would give my man the impetus of hope that he needed.

And then, although it wasn't a logical point, I felt I ought to decide in favour of anything that would help improve our home and our land because I was expecting my third baby. I hadn't said anything to anyone about it yet because I wasn't absolutely sure, but before the month was out I had no doubt.

Next day I went back to Beckindale and phoned the law

firm. 'I'd like to make an appointment to see Mr Lacey.'

'When would you like to come?'

'As soon as possible.' I felt I might get in a state again if I didn't do it quickly.

In the end I arranged to go that afternoon. This time I had to get Mrs Harper to take our Peg, but it was no problem.

The lawyer invited me to sit down and waited for me to begin.

'Mr Lacey, do you correspond back and forth about business across the Atlantic? Write letters and make phone calls?'

'Why, yes I do,' he said, rather surprised. 'As a matter of fact, I made a trans-Atlantic call last evening.'

'To report that I hadn't signed the papers and accepted the money without question.'

He sat back in his chair, rested his elbows on the arms, folded his well-manicured hands, and looked at me with a furrowed brow.

'Mrs Sugden, I fear I underrated you.'

'Happen you did. But I don't underrate you. I'd like you to pass on a message for me.'

'Certainly.'

'I'd like you to say that I accepted this money with gratitude, but though this is the first time I've expressed my thanks it's the second time I've been grateful.'

'The second time? I don't understand.'

'Never mind. That's the message.'

'It shall be done. And if there's a reply? You're not on the phone, otherwise I could ring you . . .?'

'There won't be a reply.'

'How can you know that?'

I knew it because Laurence would draw back from the situation. While he could help me without seeming to ask for gratitude, he would have gone on. But by letting him know I'd fathomed the secret, I was putting an end to it. If anyone were to ask me why I did it, I can only say I felt there were dangers in letting it go on. It would begin to seem as if I had some sort of fairy-godmother waiting to turn pumpkins into coaches for me. At least, that's how I saw it. Happen I was being over-careful – happen no one would have given it a thought. There might never have been another occasion on which Laurence would send help. But I thought it best to make an end.

Don't think I did it easily. I was very unhappy. The mere fact that I felt it so deeply was a warning. I had my husband and my family – I oughtn't to feel so much for anyone else.

Mr Lacey produced a folder with some legal documents, pressed an intercom on his desk to summon in his clerks, and we went through the performance of signatures. He then presented me with another document, which turned out to be a letter of credit.

'What do I do with this?'

'You deposit it in your bank.'

'I haven't got a bank.'

'No?' He raised his eyebrows. 'Open an account then, Mrs Sugden.'

'Thank you very much, Mr Lacey.'

'Good luck.'

'Thank you.'

When I got back to Hotten, the banks were shut. But it didn't matter any road. I'd no intention of opening an account for myself. What would my Jacob have thought? It would have been a terrible slap in the face to him, to have to ask me to write cheques for the work he wanted done. No, no, the money would go into Jacob's account, and he'd have the use of it.

There was nearly half an hour to wait for the bus to Beckindale. Some of the shops were still open. I felt the letter of credit burning a hole in my handbag. For the first time in my life I had an urge to rush into a shop and spend a lot of money, without having to stop and think whether I could afford it.

There was a sweetshop by the bus stop. Easter was coming early this year, and the shop window was full of Easter eggs in gorgeous silver paper. The shopkeeper had decorated them with little chicks made of yellow cotton wool, sitting on the handles of baskets trimmed with yellow ribbon. I suddenly thought how my little Peggy would love one of those pretty baskets even though, happen, she was a bit too young to understand what it was. And there was an Easter egg done up in a cardboard train, with a little Easter chick sitting on the chimney – my Jack would just adore it.

I was on the point of going into the shop and spending ten hard-earned shillings on those two items when a voice spoke at my elbow.

'Waiting for the bus, Annie?'

It was David Annersley. I was so pleased and elated with this feeling that I could buy what I liked for the kiddies that I put out my hand to him. 'Eh, it's nice to see you, David!'

My father might say we ought to avoid each other, but I couldn't go along with that. David had done nothing to deserve neglect – he had been a good friend to me when I needed friends, and I just couldn't turn my back on him even though Dad thought I ought to. I'd chatted to him whenever I came across him, and this was just another such occasion.

'You waiting for the bus too?'

'Aye. I've been in Hotten all day, inquiring after a job.'

'Oh? What kind of job?'

David, like his Dad, was good with machinery. He could put any tractor together again, no matter how dilapidated.

He explained that the job was with a diesel manufacturing firm that was just starting up in a new factory on the outskirts of Doncaster.

'You're leaving Beckindale, then?' I said, a bit taken aback. Somehow I'd got the notion he would always be around.

'I think it might be a good idea,' he said.

'How d'you mean?'

'Oh, various reasons . . .' He looked at me, kind of serious. It struck me he wasn't nearly as cheerful as he used to be.

'Is anything wrong, David?'

'Not with you, I can see that,' he said. 'I suppose having Jacob back makes all the difference.'

'Well, of course.' I couldn't understand what he meant. Naturally, a wife would be happier if her missing husband turned up.

'Everything all right?' he ventured. 'Jacob and you? He's . . . settling down, is he?

I shrugged. 'Jacob's not a man to settle completely,' I

confessed.

'You mean he might take off again?'

'Not if I can help it!'

'Oh, I see. You're . . . you're keen to make a go of it, are you?'

The bus arrived just then and we clambered aboard. We lost the train of our conversation but, thinking back on it much later, I realised that David was asking me if I had 'forgiven' Jacob, if I still loved him. That question was never put in so many words, and if it had been I don't know how I would have answered. For the fact was, I'd begun to see that Jacob and I weren't – as the saying goes – entirely compatible.

But what did that matter? We were man and wife, we had two children and another on the way. Whatever differences we might have, we had to put them into the background. If anyone had said to me, 'It's duty rather than love that's holding you now to Jacob,' I'd have reacted with indignation. I had a lot of affection for Jacob, and I never lost it. But I would have had to agree that the affection I felt was different from what I'd hoped to have for the man I married.

Well, what of it! How many marriages are a perfect match of heart and mind? I had come to terms with my lot, and I'll say now with absolute frankness that I never once thought of David Annersley as a way of escape from Jacob. I didn't feel that I needed to escape. I was sure I could make a go of things; even if I didn't make a hundred per cent success of it, as it proved, I tried, I always tried.

So I didn't really understand what David was saying to me then. Years later, when he came back to Beckindale, he told me that I had an 'innocence' that protected me from understanding what he was after. I think that's a strange word to use. To my mind, it wasn't so much 'innocence' as 'straightforwardness.' Like most folk, I'm no good at analysing my own character – but I do think I'm reasonably honest, reasonably straightforward. And I always believed – straightforwardly – that when David offered his help and friendship, he meant just that.

I think that on the bus journey from Hotten to Beckindale

that day, he was trying to find out if I felt resentment or indignation against Jacob. I think he wanted to know if I was— even by a little—discontented, ready to pack up and go. If I had given him any reason to think I felt like that, David Annersley might have stayed in the neighbourhood.

But the fact was, I was so taken up with what had happened in the Harrogate lawyer's office that I really didn't pay too much heed to what he was saying.

Poor lad. It must have been disheartening to him to get such short shrift. If he had only known it, the man I was thinking of most wasn't David Annersley. It wasn't even Jacob Sugden. It was Laurence. Inside myself, even when I was abstractedly replying to David's remarks, I was saying goodbye to Laurence. The message I'd given to Mr Lacey would be delivered this evening; Laurence would know that I'd guessed at his continuing interest in me. He would know that by asking Mr Lacey to say those particular words, I was telling him we must forget each other, once and for all.

I wasn't unhappy about it. I'd come to terms with that ages ago. But my thoughts were with Laurence. I wanted him to know that I had respect and affection for him still, that I wished him well from the bottom of my heart, that I hoped he'd meet someone and get married and have the blessing of children. I didn't know the expression in those days, but I suppose I was 'sending out thought-waves' to him.

So poor David Annersley was utterly wasting his time sounding me out about how I felt over Jacob. I'm sorry now that I was so taken up with myself on that occasion but, in the end, happen it was for the best.

He insisted on walking with me to the gate of Emmerdale. I couldn't understand why he should bother—he lived with his parents on the Verney estate and he'd have to retrace his steps entirely. At one point on the walk I stopped and urged him to turn back, because it was twilight and chilly.

He took my hand and looked at me. I couldn't really read his expression in the gloom. 'D'you want me to go?' he said.

'I think you'd better,' I said, answering the question I thought he was asking. 'Your mother will have your tea on the table.'

'Yes,' he said with a sigh. I had made a response that told him as much as if I'd replied to the question he was really asking, which was: Do you think I should leave Beckindale? The fact that I didn't understand what he was asking was answer enough.

He packed up and took his leave of Beckindale a couple of weeks later. I got a note from him which surprised me, though it more or less explained things that had puzzled me. I still have that note; I keep it to remind me that we shouldn't be insensitive to the unhappiness of others. That poor lad had grown far too fond of me, and I had let it happen – because, of course, I was too taken up with myself and my problems.

But that was in the future.

Now he shook hands with me, then he suddenly pulled me towards him as if he were going to kiss me. I was startled, stiffened, and stared up at him.

'Ah, lass, lass!' he sighed. 'You're the bonniest thing in the dale – and the best . . .'

'Get away wi' thee!' I said, laughing – and the moment was over.

He turned back and I went on alone, pulling my tweed coat up round my neck against the night wind. I was sending my thoughts forward to our house, thinking of how grand it would be tell my news. Of course I wasn't going to say a word about Laurence. As far as my family were concerned, this money came from Great Aunt Halbert.

I paused for a moment in the gathering darkness by the stone wall that marks our orchard. The trees still hadn't begun to bud; the weather up on our moors is too chill to see much leaf in an orchard in March. But I knew the trees would come into leaf and into fruit, and that the cycle of seasons would go on. And this year, we'd have a bit of cash to help with things that we'd had to let slide for too long.

Stars began to peep out in the sky between the branches of the apple and pear trees. I said, aloud: 'Thank you, Dear Lord, for what has happened. Thank you for giving me the friendship of a heart like Laurence's. Bless him now and for the future.'

Jacob was waiting for me with our Peg when I got indoors. He'd fetched her from the vicarage. 'Well, come on – how much?' he cried.

'Five hundred pounds.'

'Five hundred?'

'It's a lot, isn't it?' I handed him the letter of credit.

'Good old Auntie Angela,' he said, whistling with amazement. He turned the paper round in his hands for a bit then said, 'What do you want to do with it, lass?'

'You'd best bank it, hadn't you?'

'You . . . you don't want to put it in an account for yourself?'

'Nay . . . What would be the point?'

He made a sound, half a laugh and half a sigh. 'Eh, lass,' he said. Then, leaping up, 'Tell thee what! First thing we'll do wi' the money – we'll get electricity extended from t'byre to the house! How's that?'

'Jacob!'

'Would you like it?'

'*Would* I!

'Electric? Like in Mrs Soames house?' put in our Jack.

'Aye, lad – what dost think o' that?'

'Can I have an electric train set?' Jack said.

'Nay, don't let's go mad!' Jacob laughed.

'Can we have electric in time to have a television set for the Coronation?' Jack persisted.

His father went off into gales of laughter at the notion, and took the boy outside with him to look for an old clockwork train set he'd had as a boy and thought was in the barn.

Dad came in while they were gone. I thought he seemed a bit stiff in his greeting, considering he must have known there was news to tell.

'Got home all right then, did you?' he remarked.

'Well . . . as you see, Dad.'

'Oh, I saw, all right,' he said in a grim tone.

'What did you see?'

'Thee and David Annersley, that's what!' he burst out.

'Was he wi' you in Harrogate?'

'Dad!' I was genuinely shocked. 'You know very well I went to Harrogate to see the lawyer! What on earth would I want with David on a jaunt like that?'

'Then why werta comin' home arm in arm wi' him?'

'Because he happened to be on the bus coming back from Hotten! And he said he'd see me to the gate—'

'Didn't think you could find your way on your own?'

'I don't know what he thought,' I said, beginning to feel quite angry at his tone. 'I got him to turn back halfway.'

'And did you turn back halfway, an' all?'

'I don't know what you're on about,' I replied, more baffled than angry now. 'Don't you want to hear the news?'

'I'm afeared to ask it,' he said, in a sombre voice.

I was still staring at him in surprise when Jacob came bursting in with Jack.

'We're rich,' Jacob said. He waved the letter of credit under Dad's nose. 'Annie's going to have electricity! I may even buy her a vacuum cleaner!'

My father didn't catch his enthusiasm. He grunted: 'I thought first thing would be, thee'd fill in those papers for t' Ministry grant.'

'I'll do that, don't worry,' Jacob cried. 'And just think what that lass o' yours has done, Sam! — she's turned over her entire legacy to me, to use for t'farm.'

There was a pause. 'She has?' my father said.

I frowned at him. 'What else did you expect?'

'I . . . er . . . I . . . sort o' thought you had other ideas in your head these days.'

'Ideas other than t'farm?'

'You wouldn't be the first lass that got tired o' the hard life on a moorland farm.'

'Don't thee be daft,' I said. I felt a sudden surge of fondness for him. What odd idea had he got into his head? I fetched his cup and poured him a good cup of tea. He sat down, put sugar in, stirred it round and round, then said: 'Ah, sitha . . . It was getting on dark. I must' a got a wrong view of thing.'

'Of what thing?' Jack said. 'Did you see a ghost, Grandad?'

Dad laughed suddenly. 'I thought I saw an apparition from the future, lad, not a ghost from the past. But it seems I was wrong.'

Jack gaped at him. 'What's a parishon, Grandad?'

'Nowt for you to worry your noddle about,' was the reply. 'So – we're rich, are we?'

My husband was beaming. 'Take the day off tomorrow, Sam, and we'll all go for a walk round Emmerdale to see what wants doing, so's we can put it on the claim form to the Ministry.'

'Take a day off?' Dad said, astounded.

'Aye, go on, be a devil!'

'We-ell . . . happen I will, since it's a special occasion.'

Later, while Jacob and my father sat down discussing which fields to ask the Ministry surveyor to look at, I put the children to bed. Peggy was a bit fractious because she'd sensed the excitement but she settled at last. As I was saying goodnight to Jack, he put his arms round my neck.

'Will you like having a vacuum cleaner?' he asked.

'Yes, love, I'll be right pleased.'

'I'm glad, then. I don't mind about not having the train.'

'Thank you, Jack.'

'Goodnight, then.' He snuggled down. I lowered the light in the lamp. Within minutes he was asleep.

I stood for a long time in the dimness, feeling the tranquility creep into my being. Tranquility and hope . . . The house seemed full of it.

It was a long time since I'd felt this sense of hopefulness. For a while now I'd had a feeling of hovering danger from some quarter that I couldn't quite apprehend – but that was gone. I seemed to sense a new beginning tonight.

When I came downstairs the men were busy talking facts and figures. I wasn't quite ready to join in the practicalities yet. Though I'd have been embarrassed to admit it, I felt strange – happy and unhappy at the same time, strangely emotional . . .

I nodded at them and walked on to the door and out into the yard. The cold wind struck sharp on my face. The geese, sensing my presence in the darkness, gave a soft cackle of recognition. There was a square of soft yellow from the lamplight through the kitchen window. It was all very familiar, very reassuring.

A few lines of poetry came into my mind from somewhere:

Only a man harrowing clods
In a slow silent walk
With an old horse that stumbles and nods
Half asleep as they stalk.

Only thin smoke without flame
From the heaps of couch grass;
Yet this will go onward the same
Though dynasties pass . . .

Yes, 'onward the same, Though dynasties pass' – that is the farming life, its philosophy, its justification. Those words of Thomas Hardy's steadied and calmed me.

'Hey-up, lass,' my husband called. 'Come indoors, thou'lt catch thee death o' cold out there!'

With a smile to myself, I turned my back on the chill of the night and stepped into the comfortable warmth of the kitchen, where our future was being planned.